THE DRAGON DETECTIVE AGENCY

THE CASE OF THE STOLEN FILM

THE DRAGON DETECTIVE AGENCY

A

THE CASE OF THE STOLEN FILM

GARETH P. JONES

BLOOMSBURY

LONDON BERLIN NEW YORK

First published in Great Britain in 2008 by Bloomsbury Publishing Plc
36 Soho Square, London, W1D 3QY

A CIP catalogue record of this book is available from the British Library

ISBN 978 0 7475 9554 0

Typeset by Dorchester Typesetting Group Ltd
Printed in Great Britain by Clays Ltd, St Ives Plc

3 5 7 9 10 8 6 4 2

www.bloomsbury.com

FSC
Mixed Sources
Product group from well-managed
forests and other controlled sources
Cert no. SGS-COC-2061
www.fsc.org
© 1996 Forest Stewardship Council

For Charlotte, so far away
And Stanley and Ethan, much nearer

Chapter One

Brant Buchanan kicked off his expensive shoes, loosened his silk tie and reclined in the plush leather back seats of his customised Bentley, identical to the one he used in the UK, except for the US licence plates and the steering wheel on the left.

'LA is far too hot,' he said as the air conditioning kicked in, bringing the temperature down to a bearable level. 'Please tell me you've discovered something, Weaver.'

His driver flicked a switch that made his face appear on the plasma screen in front of Mr Buchanan. 'I have located two gentlemen who should be able to help,' he replied.

The silver-haired billionaire smiled at the image of his most trusted employee. 'I knew you wouldn't let me down,' he said warmly.

'But I should warn you, they are a little eccentric,' added Weaver.

'Given the subject matter, I would expect nothing less,' said Buchanan.

Buchanan pushed one of the many glowing buttons in the car door and a panel opened. He reached in and pulled out a book. It was a red hardback with a white zigzag across the cover. If there had ever been a dust jacket, it had long since been lost. There was no title or author's name on the cover but, as Brant opened the book, on the first page were the words:

DRAGONLORE
A Scientific Study of Dragons
By Ivor Klingerflim

'This is such a fascinating book, Weaver,' said Buchanan. 'For example, did you know that dragon mothers plant their eggs in the liquid fires of earth's Inner Core then wait on the banks for the young dragons to swim to the surface?'

'No, sir, I didn't, sir,' replied Weaver, whose lack of

enthusiasm for his boss's latest project hadn't stopped him carrying out his orders efficiently and unquestioningly. It was he who had scoured the world for the book before discovering this copy in a charity shop in North London.

'Listen to this bit,' said Mr Buchanan, reading from the book. *"The term up-airer relates to a great Himalayan conference, held a thousand or so years ago, when those dragons in favour of destroying mankind rose into the air (and became known as up-airers). Luckily for humans, the majority stayed on the ground and so dragonkind went into hiding."'*

'Fascinating, sir,' said Weaver.

Mr Buchanan continued to read out loud. *"In spite of this, many dragons believe that war between humans and dragons is inevitable and that they will be led into battle by a dragon carrying the Turning Stone, a large spherical rock which is said to give power over all dragonkind."'*

'Shall I take you back to Sands Hall?' said Weaver, starting the engine and slipping the control stick into drive.

'Yes, please,' replied Buchanan.

Light classical music filled the car.

'It may take some time. The traffic in LA is particularly bad this evening.'

9

'That's because no one walks in this city,' replied Buchanan.

He pressed a button and a drink appeared from the side door. He pushed another and the image of Weaver's face was replaced by a piece of grainy CCTV footage. Buchanan picked up the drink and sat back to watch. It showed an office from three different angles. A dragon dropped into the room, looked around and then reached up and lowered a young girl in too.

'Shouldn't we be using her to get to the dragon?' said Weaver. 'There's clearly a connection between them.'

'In business I always find it best to arm myself with as much information as possible before making an acquisition,' replied Buchanan, 'but yes, perhaps it is time to make good use of young Holly Bigsby.'

Chapter Two

On the other side of the Atlantic, a red-backed, green-bellied, urban-based Mountain Dragon called Dirk Dilly was crouching on the roof of a building across the road from a warehouse in East London, perfectly camouflaged against its red tiles.

A high wire fence surrounded the warehouse and two others with a sign that read 'DANGER: DEMOLITION IN PROGRESS'. A fourth warehouse had already been reduced to rubble, except for its back wall. Within the fenced area were a number of workmen wearing yellow bibs and hard hats. One of them was operating a large red machine that looked like an enormous crab's claw attached to the base of a tank.

He pulled a lever and the claw crashed into the remaining wall of the destroyed building. The claw snapped shut, crushing bricks and sending clouds of dust into the air.

That morning, as usual, Dirk had been watching a skyscraper in London called Centrepoint, which he had recently learnt was used as a base by Vainclaw Grandin's Kinghorns, a group of dragons who were intent on waging war against humans.

Several weeks had passed without seeing one dragon until finally today he had spotted one on top of the building, silhouetted against the night sky.

Dirk had remained where he was, watching from a safe distance. The dragon came to the edge of the building, checked no one was looking, spread its wings and glided down, sailing over Dirk's head and landing on a nearby church. It was the Sea Dragon, Flotsam, one of the original gang of four Kinghorns that Dirk had discovered in London.

Flotsam moved swiftly across the roofs. Dirk followed. Heading east, the Sea Dragon had gone into the same warehouse the four Kinghorns had used when Dirk first discovered their presence in London, only now it was being knocked down.

The foreman blew a whistle.

'Tea's up,' he shouted and all the workmen, including the one operating the claw, headed towards a cabin on the far side of the site.

Dirk took his opportunity and leapt from the rooftop, spreading his wings, touching a foot on the top of the machine, spring-boarding up into the air and landing on the flat roof of the warehouse.

He peered in through the dirty skylight.

Below were the four crates he had seen before with the words 'DO NOT OPEN' printed in red on the top. In the middle of the crates was a Mountain Dragon – red-backed and green-bellied just like himself. It was Jegsy Grandin, nephew of Vainclaw. Flotsam was standing to one side.

Dirk opened the skylight and slipped inside, closing it behind him as quietly as possible and blending with the rafters.

He looked down.

Jegsy had plugged an old-fashioned record player into a wall, causing the turntable to rotate. In place of a record he had balanced a long-stemmed lamp-stand on top of a silver hubcap of a car. As the stand spun round, he tried to add a yellow hard hat, like the ones worn by the workmen outside. Moving ever so slowly, Jegsy placed the hat on top and, for a second, it looked like he had succeeded in this pointless goal. Jegsy watched, transfixed. Then the hat began to wobble violently, tipping the lamp-stand and sending it and the hubcap crashing to the floor.

'So close,' said Jegsy, picking up the bits.

'Jegsy, you idiot, that's enough, like. We've got to get out of here,' said Flotsam. 'They're going to knock this place down.'

'But Vainclaw said to stay here,' protested Jegsy.

'Listen, Jegs, I just had a word with the boss and there's been a change of plan. We got new orders.'

'I haven't heard anything.'

'That's because you're too busy playing with your stupid toys.'

'Eh, calm down,' said Jegsy. 'These aren't toys. They're useful things. I just haven't figured out what they're used for yet.'

'Aw, come on, even I know that humans wear the yellow bowls on their soft heads so that they don't get hurt. Look.' Flotsam picked up the hard hat and jammed it over Jegsy's head then spun around and whacked him with his tail, sending him flying across the room.

Jegsy stood up and dusted himself down. He touched the hard hat on his head then smiled. 'Oh yeah, cheers, Flotsam,' he said, pleased with the discovery.

'Look, Jegs, we're mates, ain't we?' said the Sea Dragon. 'The Dragnet are hunting Kinghorns. They've even got a couple of officers watching the underground entrance to this place.'

'Dragnet officers?' said Jegsy, sounding concerned.

'Yeah, but don't worry. I've just done a deal that will give us safe passage but we've got to get moving.'

'But Vainclaw said –'

'I told you, I got new orders. Now come on,' snapped Flotsam.

Outside, the house-crushing machine started up again and the shouts of the workmen could be heard. There was an enormous crash, which shook the building so violently that the colour returned to Dirk's skin for a moment. Luckily, neither Jegsy nor Flotsam noticed.

The red metal of the large claw came through the side of the building. It withdrew, causing bits of brick to fall down. One of them landed on top of Jegsy's head, bouncing off his hard hat and whacking Flotsam in the face.

'Eh, you're right about the yellow bowl,' said Jegsy. 'I didn't feel a thing.'

'Come on, you idiot,' snarled Flotsam, jumping into a crate. 'I'm getting out of here. Are you coming or not?'

'Eh, watch who you're calling an idiot,' replied Jegsy, grabbing the record player and jumping into another crate. They both spoke a few words in Dragonspeak, asking the rock to take them down. The rock, being rock, took them down into the ground.

A second crash rocked the building. Dirk lost his grip and fell to the ground. Bits of wood and concrete landed on top of him. The machine had made a large hole in the corner of the building. Dirk jumped up and shook the dust off his back. He ran around the crates, knocking them away. Beneath each one was a patch of solid rock. They would all lead to an entrance deep beneath the foundations of London, but Dirk couldn't afford to bump into the Dragnet officers that Flotsam had mentioned. Drakes weren't too discriminating in who they arrested. The last time Dirk had bumped into some, he had wound up in prison. He had managed to escape with the help of a Sea Dragon called Alba Longs and a yellow-bellied, coal-black Cave Dweller called Fairfax Nordstrum, but it had been close and he didn't fancy repeating the experience.

There was a terrible scraping as the machine

chewed away at the building. Dirk ran to a window. It was boarded up but he could see traces of yellow from the workmen's bibs through the slats. He checked the other sides. He was surrounded. He thought fast. He had once seen a documentary on demolishing buildings and remembered how the voice-over had said that it was vital that the electricity, gas and water supplies be turned off.

'Rats in a basket,' exclaimed Dirk, 'that's it.'

Jegsy had plugged in the record player, so if the electricity hadn't been disconnected, maybe some of the other supplies had been left on.

Dirk searched the walls and found a small gas heater in the corner. A metal pipe ran into the back of it from the wall. He yanked it away. Escaping gas hissed. Dirk held a paw over it. He deftly lifted an overturned crate with his tail, grabbed it with his free paw and pushed it over the pipe, releasing the end so that the gas filled the crate.

There was another CRASH! as the crunching machine came though a window. Dirk could hear the workmen shouting. He had to act quickly before they got too close. He didn't want anyone to get hurt.

The smell of gas seeped through the gaps of the crate. The crunching machine took hold of a section of the building and twisted, mangling a mass of metal rods that ran through the wall. The whole structure shook, causing the skylight to crack and shards of glass to shower on to Dirk. He flew up to the hole in the roof.

'Here goes nothing,' he said.

He looked down at the crate, took aim, opened his mouth and exhaled. A line of fire shot down into the warehouse, catching the escaping vapours of gas, drawing flames down into the crate. It seemed like there was a moment's silence, like an intake of breath, before it happened.

At the top of his voice, Dirk shouted, 'Take cover!'

There was a flash of light. The sound of the explosion filled the air and the surrounding workmen dived to the ground to protect themselves from the blast.

Lying down, covering their faces, none of them noticed the four-metre-long, red-backed, green-bellied, urban-based Mountain Dragon flying over their heads.

Chapter Three

Holly was imprisoned in her house for the whole of the summer. The last time she had been out, she had returned home late at night, her jeans torn and covered in blood but with no visible sign of injury. Dad's big-haired wife had demanded to know where she had been and what had happened but she couldn't very well tell them the truth: that her leg had been broken flying up an elevator shaft on a Mountain Dragon's back, then fixed by a Sky Dragon called Nebula Colorado.

So she said nothing and as punishment for her irresponsible behaviour they had grounded her for the whole summer holiday.

No TV, no computer and no leaving the house until school began in September. The external doors and windows were kept locked at all times using keys that Big Hair kept on her bedside table at night. Even if she could get the keys and open the doors, there was no way of deactivating the alarm without the four-digit code, which changed every week.

At least Archie was allowed to visit. Dad and Big Hair let him come round because they thought it was a good sign that Holly had made a friend at last. Holly and Archie spent most of their time in her room messing about. Sometimes they played hide-and-seek, with Holly using her ability to blend with her surroundings, a skill she had picked up from accidentally tasting dragon blood. They talked about dragons. Archie's favourite story was the time Vainclaw Grandin had entranced the whole of Little Hope Village Hall in order to force the Prime Minister to operate a secret government weapon, which Vainclaw had learnt about from Callum Thackley, the Prime Minister's son.

'Poor Callum,' Holly said the last time she recounted the story.

'But he was on their side, wasn't he?' Archie argued.

'Yeah, but Vainclaw drove him mad with Dragonsong. All the psychiatrists think the monsters are in his head, but they're not, are they?' Holly didn't mention that Callum still wrote to her, strange tortured letters about monsters and madness. She always read them in case there was any indication that Vainclaw had been back in touch, but they scared her.

Archie remembered his own experience of dragons and nodded. Then he said, 'Nebula was amazing, wasn't she? What do you think she meant when she told you that she was part of you now?'

'Well, she used her own ash to fix my leg, didn't she?' replied Holly.

'Does it feel any different?'

Holly stood up. 'No, just the same.'

'Try hopping,' said Archie.

Holly hopped. 'It just feels like the other leg.'

'Hop for the rest of the day – see what happens,' said Archie, grinning.

'You want me to see what it feels like if I kick you?' replied Holly, chasing him round on one leg.

'No thanks,' said Archie, laughing.

Archie's visits were all Holly had to look forward to, but he hadn't been round for days. Holly felt like a caged animal, which was why she had taken to sneaking downstairs to watch TV late at night while Dad and Big Hair were asleep.

21

She slipped into the front room, turned on the TV and instantly muted it. She couldn't afford to wake them. They had made it perfectly clear what would happen if she was discovered out of her room.

'One step out of line and I'm sending you back to William Scrivener's,' Dad had said.

Holly had hated her time at the rich-kid boarding school, sharing a room with Petal Moses, away from London, away from Willow, her cat, and away from Dirk.

She turned the volume on quietly and flicked through the channels. It was the usual late-night programming: live-streaming of a reality TV show showing a bunch of people sleeping, an American detective film and an unfunny sitcom. Holly stopped on a channel showing a female presenter with tangerine-coloured skin and a smile set to full beam, sitting behind a desk with *Hollywood Gossip* written behind her.

'What are your children doing this summer?' chirruped the presenter happily. 'Whatever it is, I bet it won't be as exciting as it is for one very special twelve-year-old, currently here in Hollywood making a movie all about herself. It could only be Petal Moses, pop's most precocious offspring.'

A picture of Petal appeared behind her. She looked different from the time Holly had shared a room with her at William Scrivener's School. She had a healthy tan, her hair had been cut into a trendy new style and she was sporting a nose ring.

'The movie in question? It's the adaptation of Petal's autobiography, *When Petals Blossom*. The film, called *Petal – The Movie*, will star young Miss Moses in the title role and will be directed by legendary Hollywood film director Chase Lampton.'

A man with thick curly black hair, wearing sunglasses and a leather jacket, appeared on the screen. 'To me it's more than a movie about the child of a pop star slash actress,' said the man. 'It's kind of an analysis of celebrity culture.'

It cut back to the presenter. 'Lampton will also be directing his own son, Dante Lampton,' she said, as the picture behind her showed the director standing next to a boy who looked like a scaled-down version of him. 'And talking of keeping things in the family, can you guess who's providing the soundtrack as well as picking up an executive producer credit? Of course, it's Petal's famous mother . . .'

Holly switched channels. She hated Petal. The spoilt pop star's daughter got everything she ever wanted and probably always would. Holly wasn't jealous that Petal was making a film or that she was in Hollywood but she did envy her freedom.

Hearing the door creak, she quickly switched off the TV and froze, blending with the sofa, but the footsteps that entered the room were too light to be Dad or Big Hair. Holly's head reappeared as she turned to see a black cat with a white face and a black smudge on her nose padding into the room. She reached down and scooped her up.

'Hello, Willow,' she said, stroking her and noticing that her fur was cold. 'You've been outside, have you?' she said into her ear. 'Lucky thing.'

Willow miaowed in reply and Holly noticed something attached to her collar. It was a biro case but instead of a pen inside there was a rolled-up piece of paper.

'What have you got here?' asked Holly, removing the biro and pulling out the piece of paper. She unfurled it and read the note scrawled in capital letters:

COME TO THE CAT FLAP

Holly muted the TV and crept to the kitchen. She

crouched down and looked through the cat flap to find Archie Snellgrove's blue eyes blinking back at her, his unkempt dirty blond hair falling over his face.

'What are you doing here?' she asked.

'Can I come in? It's really cold,' said Archie, shivering as he spoke.

Chapter Four

Back in the safety of his top-floor office, Dirk sat back, his feet on the desk, sipping a cocktail of orange and blackcurrant squash. On the TV was one of his all-time favourite films, *The Big Zero*. It was one of the classic American detective films. It was the reason Dirk had become a detective in the first place. He blew a smoke ring and relaxed.

'Mr Dilly, are you awake?' whispered a shaky voice from outside his door.

'Wide awake, Mrs Klingerflim,' said Dirk.

The door opened and his elderly landlady's owl-like face appeared.

'Sorry to bother you so late, Mr Dilly,' she said.

'I've always got time for you, Mrs K,' he replied.

'Oh, you are sweet,' said Mrs Klingerflim, removing her thick glasses and wiping the lenses. Dirk noticed how old and fragile she looked without them. She put them back on and said, 'That's better, now I can see you.'

For years, Dirk had assumed that Mrs Klingerflim was so blind that she thought he was human. It had come as a complete surprise to learn that she knew not only that he was a dragon, but his exact sub-species, due to having spent years dragon-spotting with her late husband, Ivor. She had even helped write his definitive guide to dragons.

'I was worried you might be sleeping,' said the old lady. 'My dear Ivor was a very light sleeper. He used to say that a whispering ant could wake him up,' she said, shaking her head fondly. 'I'm the complete opposite. An elephant with a foghorn couldn't rouse me. Ivor used to wake me up by putting on Glen Miller records at full blast. That was on my old gramophone, of course. These days it's all electronological music played on computers, isn't it? CDs and empty threes and whatnot. It's funny how things change. I imagine one day we'll be able to stick our fingers up our noses and music will start playing.'

'Sorry, Mrs K, did you want me for something?' replied Dirk, assuming that she hadn't popped in to give him her theory on the future of music production.

'Oh yes, I'm sorry. Things fly in and out of my head like paper aeroplanes sometimes,' she said. 'Would you mind checking the cellar? There's a funny noise. I'm worried we might have rats in there or something. I'd go down myself but the steps are very steep and the doctor says I shouldn't take any unnecessary risks at my age, what with my knees and ankles.'

On the TV, two men were watching a burning building.

'Hold on, my favourite line is coming up,' said Dirk.

'I used to love the movies,' said Mrs Klingerflim. 'What's this one about, then?'

'They're brothers who run a detective agency. That was their office. You find out later that the one on the right, Chuck Tanner, paid someone to burn it down, but we don't know that yet,' said Dirk.

There was a close-up of the man, his craggy face reflecting the flickering yellow light from the fire. As he spoke, Dirk said the line along with him.

'You realise, Joe, that everything we worked for over these past ten years has just gone up in smoke?

Let's go get a bagel.'

'Brilliant,' said Dirk, following Mrs Klingerflim out of the room and down the stairs.

'This is very kind of you,' she said.

As usual, Dirk was careful to make sure his scaly skin didn't knock off the photos that lined the wall. He glanced at them as he slowly followed Mrs Klingerflim down and noticed a picture of his landlady when much younger, standing in front of a large rock, smiling at the camera. She had her arms linked with a man who had a wide grin, deep dimples and kind eyes.

'Is this Ivor?' he asked, realising that, after all his landlady had told him about her husband, he didn't even know what he looked like.

Mrs Klingerflim turned round and climbed back up one stair. She pulled the picture off the wall and squinted at it. Like a number of others, it had a scratch across it. She turned it around and read the back at arm's length.

'Oh, that's right,' she said, 'that was one of our little holidays. They were happy days. I do miss him, Mr Dilly.'

Dirk felt uncomfortable. He wasn't used to human feelings. Things were simpler for dragons. What family

29

connections existed were easily severed. Dragons didn't fall in love or get married. Even mothers didn't hang around for long.

'So, the cellar,' he said awkwardly.

'Yes, the cellar,' said Mrs Klingerflim, pulling herself out of her thoughts.

They continued in silence to the bottom of the stairs and round the corner to the cellar door. Dirk pushed it open and looked down.

'I can't hear anything,' he said.

'It comes and goes,' replied Mrs Klingerflim.

'I'll go and have a look. Where's the light switch?' he asked.

'It's on the wall, but it won't do you any good. The bulb's blown. I've been meaning to change it but the doctor said I shouldn't be standing on chairs and things with my hips.'

'No problem, I'll make my own light,' said Dirk, opening his mouth to breathe fire.

'I'd rather you didn't,' said the old lady, 'only there are a few things with sentimental value down there, and I fear they may be rather flammable. I've found you a torch.'

She handed him a black plastic torch. Dirk switched it on and headed down the cellar stairs.

In the cellar, he swung the torch around. There were boxes full of notebooks and scraps of paper. He picked up a notepad from under a curved paperweight and flicked through it. It was full of sketches of dragons.

'What is all this stuff?' he shouted up the stairs.

'It's Ivor's notes for the book. I know it's silly but I couldn't bear to throw them away.'

Dirk stopped at a page with a line drawing of a dragon with hundreds of thin spikes covering its back. At the bottom of the page Ivor had written: *Californian Desert Dragon – 1973.*

'Can you hear anything now?' called Mrs Klingerflim.

'Nothing yet,' said Dirk. 'What sort of noise was it?'

'It sounded like a kind of scratching.'

Dirk placed the notepad back on the pile and looked around.

'There it goes,' said Mrs Klingerflim.

Dirk listened. Sure enough, the old girl's eyesight might have been failing but her hearing was fine. There was a quiet scratching coming from beneath a faded wooden dressing table in a dark corner of the cellar.

Dirk moved quietly to the dressing table and gently eased out the bottom drawer. He was bracing himself

31

for rats. Dirk wasn't a big fan of rats, but the pair of eyes was too big to belong to a rat and the skin was scaly rather than furry.

'Hi, Dirk,' whispered Karnataka Cuddlums, his unreliable friend.

'Have you found anything, Mr Dilly?' called Mrs Klingerflim.

Dirk looked down at the Shade-Hugger's brown head inside the base of the dressing table.

'It's just as we thought,' he shouted. 'A rat.'

Chapter Five

Archie looked freezing.

'I can't open the door,' said Holly. 'They're alarmed. You know how serious they are about keeping me in.'

'I could climb in through a window,' he suggested.

'The whole place is shut up like a prison. You have to go home,' insisted Holly. 'If they find you here now, they won't let you visit any more.'

'I can't go home,' he said.

'Why?'

Archie stared back at her stubbornly. Holly could tell that he wasn't going to answer her question but over the short time that they had known each other she had learnt to trust him.

'Are you telling me that they've locked this place up so tightly that even the great Holly Bigsby can't get round it?' said Archie, with a challenging smile.

'Well . . .' Holly smiled back. 'Stay there,' she said, letting go of the cat flap and making her way up the stairs.

As it happened, Holly had worked out a way around her parents' precautions. She had no intention of carrying it out. It was just something to do. But as long as she could get Archie in and out unnoticed, Dad and Big Hair would be none the wiser.

At night Big Hair kept the keys on her bedside table. Last week, Holly had overheard her and Dad arguing about it.

'But, Bridget, what if there's a fire?' her dad had said. 'Isn't it a bit dangerous?'

'The most dangerous thing in this house is that daughter of yours,' she had replied. 'It's time to rein her in unless you want a delinquent on your hands.'

Holly had wanted her dad to defend her, but as usual he just said, 'I suppose you're right, dear,' and went back to the newspaper he was reading.

'And I've come up with a way to help you remember the alarm code.' Big Hair had lowered her voice.

'I've put the number into your mobile phone.'

'Very clever, darling. Good idea,' he replied, without looking up from his paper.

Big Hair had looked pleased with herself. Then she said, 'Shouldn't you be doing some work?'

'Er . . .' Dad shifted uncomfortably. 'Brant has employed me more in an advisory capacity. He said he would let me know when he needed me.'

Holly had felt her blood boil, knowing full well that Brant Buchanan had only employed him to reveal the whereabouts of a secret government weapon. Now the billionaire had successfully stolen and used the weapon, Dad just sat around reading newspapers.

Holly's plan was to sneak into Dad and Big Hair's bedroom, remove the mobile phone from Dad's pocket and the keys from Big Hair's bedside table, deactivate the alarm, open the door and let Archie in, then reactivate the alarm, lock the door and replace the phone and keys. If she left a window unlocked, Archie could sneak out through the window in the morning and no one would ever know he was there. Simple.

Holly darted up the stairs, careful to avoid the noisy floorboards, and across the landing to the bedroom door. She pushed it open and poked her head round the corner, ever ready to freeze and blend if either of them stirred.

Her dad was snoring lightly. Big Hair was sleeping silently beside him. Holly tiptoed into the room. On a wicker chair on her dad's side lay his discarded clothes. On the back of the chair was his suit jacket. Holly checked the trouser pockets but there was no phone. She slipped around to the other side of the chair. Her dad muttered something in his sleep. She froze, but he didn't wake up so Holly carefully picked up the suit jacket and reached into the inside pocket, pulling out the mobile phone. She slipped it into her own pocket and moved swiftly to the other side of the bed.

Big Hair was sleeping with her face disconcertingly near to where the keys rested on the bedside table. Holly approached. She noticed that Big Hair's eyes were only half shut. For a moment she thought that she was awake, but she quickly realised that her eyes weren't focusing on her and from the rhythmic breathing it was clear that she was asleep.

Holly reached inside her T-shirt and pulled out the dragon claw she had taken to wearing round her neck, having threaded a piece of string through a hole in it. She knew it was risky to carry around proof of dragon existence but she wore it because it reminded her of the world that had opened up to her since meeting Dirk. She used it to hook the key ring and lift it from the table before clasping a hand over the keys to stop them jangling together. Big Hair let out a small moan. 'Yes, we're thinking of having it refurbished,' she muttered in her sleep. Holly could feel her heart pounding against her chest and the blood rushing through her ears so noisily that she began to worry that if the keys didn't wake Big Hair, the sound of her own fear would, but Big Hair rolled over, still asleep.

Holly carefully placed the keys in her pocket and made her way across the room, out of the door, and down the stairs, where she pulled out her dad's mobile and unlocked it. The screen lit up and she read:

You have 78 missed calls

She OK'd the message and searched through her dad's contacts until she found Mr A Code.

'Mr A Code,' she said to herself, smiling. 'Alarm code. Subtle!'

Sure enough, Mr Code's telephone number was only four digits long. She opened the cupboard under the stairs where the alarm was kept and typed the numbers into the keypad. The alarm let out a long beep to indicate that it had been switched off.

Holly ran to the back door, unlocked it and opened it.

'Under five minutes – not bad,' said Archie, looking at his watch.

'Shh,' hushed Holly. 'Go to the front room.'

She shut the door behind Archie and locked it before following him into the room.

'Do you know how much trouble I'm in if we're found out?' she said.

Archie reached into his pocket and offered Holly a jelly bean.

'No thanks,' she said.

'Sorry. I had nowhere else to go.'

'Stay here,' she said, unlocking a window. 'I'm going to put everything back then I'll come back down again.'

'You want help?' offered Archie.

'It's easier alone. I'll be back in a second,' replied Holly, slipping back out into the hallway, up the stairs and into the bedroom.

This time she did everything in reverse, replacing the keys on the bedside table first then crossing the room and dropping the mobile phone into the jacket pocket. She turned to leave but a buzzing noise stopped her. It was the phone vibrating, rattling against the wicker chair. Her dad murmured in his sleep. Scared that it would wake him up, Holly reached back inside the pocket and lifted it out, to turn it off. On the screen were three words that made Holly's blood run cold.

Brant Buchanan calling

She hit the cancel button. The screen now read, *79 missed calls*. She felt a hand on her shoulder. She looked around to see her dad standing behind her, staring angrily at her.

'Holly, what on earth are you doing?' he whispered.

Chapter Six

Dirk raised a claw to his lips to indicate to Karnataka to stay quiet.

'Do you want a cup of tea, Mr Dilly?' called Mrs Klingerflim from upstairs.

'Yes, please,' he responded. 'Two sugars, please, Mrs K.'

He waited until he heard the old lady shuffle away to the kitchen and switch on the radio before addressing the Shade-Hugger.

'This is interesting behaviour for the Captain of Dragnet,' he said in a hushed voice, 'or have the councillors finally seen sense and sacked you?'

'Sacked me?' whined Karnataka. 'They're talking

about giving me a special commendation.'

Dirk couldn't help but smile. 'All this time you've spent on the wrong side of the law and it turns out you're better suited to working for the right side,' he said.

'I know,' said his old friend, with a shrug. 'Who'd have thought it?'

'So you're an honest dragon these days, are you?' Dirk asked sceptically.

'I'm doing the job well,' insisted Karnataka.

Dirk gave his old friend a look of disbelief.

'Well, of course, being Captain there are still plenty of opportunities to make an extra bit of gold to . . . you know . . . supplement my wage.'

Dirk smiled. 'I'm relieved. For a minute there I thought you'd gone all respectable on me,' he said.

'Come on, it's not just me – every Drake in the Dragnet is looking for a backhander.'

'No wonder you fit in so well,' said Dirk.

'Look, I'd appreciate it if you didn't go shooting your mouth off about certain things.'

'You mean like the time you stole the council's Welsh gold reserves?'

'Exactly. I'm a changed dragon.'

'I find that difficult to believe, since I currently find

you in my landlady's cellar with your head jammed inside a cheap Edwardian dressing table. What are you doing here?'

'I came to find you. The rock brought me most of the way but these human settlements have concrete foundations. You ever tried talking to concrete? It's a very one-sided conversation, I can tell you. So I had to claw my way through. Give me a hand, will you?'

'My heart bleeds. You shouldn't be here,' said Dirk.

Crackly old jazz music drifted downstairs and Dirk could hear Mrs Klingerflim shuffling around the kitchen, singing along to whatever the tune was.

'Neither of us should be here,' said Karnataka. 'I don't need to remind you that lodging with a human is a blatant breach of the forbidden divide. If you ever found yourself in front of the Dragon Council, you'd be banished to the earth's Inner Core quicker than you could say liquorice laces. Now, please help me up, Dirk, I need to speak to you properly.'

'Oh, all right, then.' Dirk gave in and lifted the dressing table away, revealing the hole that Karnataka had made in the bottom of Mrs Klingerflim's basement. He reached down and grabbed a claw that the Shade-Hugger had forced into the room, then, with an almighty tug, yanked him into the cellar. Bits of

42

concrete flew all over the place and Dirk fell backwards, as the full weight of the Shade-Hugger landed on top of him.

'Get off me,' snarled Dirk.

Karnataka jumped off but landed on the dressing table, crushing it under his weight, sending splintered wood everywhere.

'Is everything all right down there, Mr Dilly?' called Mrs Klingerflim from the top of the stairs.

'Fine, Mrs K. I just slipped.'

'Please be careful, Mr Dilly,' she said nervously. 'I know it all looks like rubbish but there are lots of things that are very valuable to me down there. My mother gave me that dressing table as a wedding gift.'

Dirk looked at the dressing table, which was utterly destroyed. 'OK, Mrs K,' he said.

'I'll leave your cup of tea at the top of the stairs here,' she said.

'She got any liquorice?' asked Karnataka, taking in his surroundings. He lifted a piece of paper. 'Hey, this looks like an Amphiptere,' he said, holding up a line drawing of a snake-like creature with a huge lion-like mane. 'What is all this stuff?'

'This stuff is none of your business,' said Dirk, snatching it from him. 'Why are you here, Karny?'

'What do you know about Minertia?' asked Karnataka.

'Just the usual. Minertia Tidfell was the oldest, wisest and greatest dragon of all. She was the one who called the great conference and counted the vote and announced that dragons would go into hiding. She defined the three aspects of the forbidden divide as being seen by a human, attacking a human or allowing a human to find any evidence of the existence of dragons. Then years later she was convicted of breaching it and banished to an eternity in the Inner Core.'

'Did you ever meet her?'

'No. I saw her at the great conference but I was pretty young then. What's all this about?' said Dirk.

'A dragon that old and powerful must have accumulated a fair amount of treasure, don't you think?' Karnataka's yellow eyes seemed to turn gold, as though reflecting all that imagined wealth.

'Ah, I knew it. It's about gold. Is this one of those opportunities to . . . how did you put it? Supplement your wage?'

'No,' protested Karnataka. 'The Kinghorns are gathering support but my spies tell me that there's a splinter group called the One-Worlders. Vainclaw is worried.'

'So? What's that got to do with Minertia's treasure?' asked Dirk.

'Vainclaw's cronies are looking for it. I guess he's looking for gold to buy support.'

'Nice try,' said Dirk, smiling wryly, 'but I've known you too long, Karny. You want to make a little extra gold for yourself.'

'A little extra gold? We're not talking about a high street jeweller's. We're talking the biggest stash of gold in the world. I've been looking through the records from her trial. Did you know the council offered to reduce her sentence if she told them where it was?'

'If no one's found it in all the years that she's been banished, I'm guessing it's pretty well hidden.'

'That's why I need you,' said Karnataka. 'Please, Dirk. You're the best there is.'

'No.'

Karnataka let out a frustrated growl. 'Seriously, if you knew what I know, knowing you, you'd be looking for it too.'

'Then tell me what you know,' said Dirk.

'That's the thing,' snorted Karnataka. 'If you knew what I know, you wouldn't help me find it.'

'Karny, I'm in no mood for your riddles. If you've nothing more to say, you can disappear down your hole and get back to your shady dealings.'

'You're making a big mistake, Dirk,' said Karnataka, but he climbed back into the hole, leaving Dirk alone in the empty cellar. Dirk picked up the bits of the dressing table and looked at it. It was way beyond repair. He piled the remains over the hole and went back up the stairs.

Chapter Seven

Mr Bigsby didn't speak as he motioned Holly and Archie into the back of the car. When the radio came on automatically, he switched it off, filling the car with an uncomfortable absence of sound.

They arrived at Sidney Clavel Estate and Mr Bigsby stopped the car and switched off the engine. Holly had only been there once before. She was struck by how much gloomier, dirtier and rougher it was than the street where she lived.

'You'd better know I intend to have a serious word with your father,' said Mr Bigsby.

'You might have to wait a while,' said Archie defiantly. 'Dad's in prison.'

For a moment Mr Bigsby looked thrown by this, then he said, 'Your mother, then.'

'Mum's . . .' Archie's voice faded away as though unsure how to finish the sentence.

They all stepped out of the car and Mr Bigsby marched them over a patch of grass, which was littered with bits of rubbish, discarded clothes and plastic bags. The area was lit by dim yellow lights. In the middle were a couple of upside-down supermarket trolleys and a mangled bicycle.

'I'm sorry, Hol,' whispered Archie.

'No talking,' barked Mr Bigsby.

Archie led them to the block where he lived, past a lift with an 'Out of Order' sign on it and up the grimy concrete stairs, which had threatening graffiti scrawled across the walls.

On the third floor they followed Archie along an outside walkway. On the floor above someone was playing music extremely loudly, and below a couple could be heard arguing. Archie stopped in front of a green door.

'This is where I live. Thanks for the lift. I'll see you later,' he said, as casually as if he was being dropped off after a trip to the cinema.

'We'll see you in,' said Mr Bigsby, waiting for him to

open the door. 'You have a key, do you?'

Archie pulled out a key from his pocket but still didn't try to open the door. 'I'll be fine from here,' he said.

'Open the door,' ordered Mr Bigsby firmly.

Archie looked pleadingly at Holly. She could tell that he didn't want to open it.

'Come on, Dad, we don't want to disturb anyone,' she said.

'Open the door,' Mr Bigsby repeated sternly.

Seeing no way to avoid it, Archie unlocked the door. 'Bye, then,' he said.

Mr Bigsby pushed the door open and switched the light on. The hallway was a mess. Pictures lay smashed on the ground, a telephone table was on its side and the telephone ripped from the wall.

'What on earth?' Mr Bigsby stepped inside.

Holly looked at Archie but he refused to meet her gaze.

They followed Mr Bigsby along the hallway into the front room, which was in as bad a state as the hallway. The sofa was on its side, scraps of paper and old magazines lay strewn across the floor and Holly noticed that the frosted glass in the door was cracked.

'She's not usually so bad,' Archie said. 'Sometimes

she's a great mum, you know, laughing and joking and messing about. Other times she gets all miserable and it's like nothing you can say or do will cheer her up. But recently she started getting really angry and shouting horrible stuff. I hid because I knew that it wouldn't be long before she'd get over it and start crying again but she carried on screaming and it was late and I suppose one of the neighbours called the police and they couldn't calm her down, so they took her away. Sectioned is what they call it. It's when they have to lock you up because you've gone wrong in the head. They would have taken me too but I ran . . .'

Tears fell down his face and Holly became aware of her own eyes welling up. She swallowed hard to avoid crying and turned to her dad, who had gone quiet.

'Come on,' he said gently.

'Where are we going?' said Holly.

'We're going home,' he replied. 'All of us.'

They returned in silence.

As Mr Bigsby turned the car into Elliot Drive, Holly noticed that another car had taken the space in front of their house. Grumbling to himself, her dad parked a few doors down.

'You'll stay with us tonight, Archie,' he said, switching off the engine. 'It's late. I'll decide what to do with you tomorrow.'

'Thanks,' said Archie, getting out and accidentally slamming the door behind him.

'Be quiet,' Mr Bigsby said, scowling. 'And utter silence on the way in. Believe me, you do not want Bridget to wake up.'

'I think it might be too late,' said Holly. 'We didn't leave the hall light on, did we?'

As she said it, the living-room light came on too. Through the net curtains they saw the silhouette of a man.

'It's a burglar,' gasped Holly.

'No it's not,' replied her dad, stopping in front of the car that was parked in his space. Holly recognised it too. It was Brant Buchanan's customised Bentley.

Holly's dad marched them all to the front door. As he opened it, Brant Buchanan's driver, Weaver, stepped into the hallway. His appearance was no less smart than usual considering the lateness of the hour. His black hair looked as if it had been painted on and his grey suit, shirt and tie matched his slip-on shoes exactly.

Big Hair's voice came from the kitchen. 'How do you take your coffee, Mr Weaver?'

Weaver nodded a cursory greeting at Mr Bigsby then looked at Holly and Archie unsmilingly. 'Black, no sugar,' he responded. 'And it's just Weaver.'

Big Hair appeared holding two mugs of coffee. She was wearing a white dressing gown. Her hair looked messy from sleep. 'I can't think where Malcolm could have got to . . .' Seeing her husband she stopped. Her gaze fell on Holly. 'I should have known you would have something to do with it,' she said.

'It wasn't Holly's fault,' said her dad. 'Now, Holly, take Archie upstairs. He can sleep in the spare room tonight.'

'Sleep in the spare room?' said Big Hair.

'I'll explain in a minute,' replied her husband. 'Sorry, Weaver, what can I do for you?'

'You're required in America immediately,' said the grey man.

'You're going to America?' said Holly.

'Actually, Mr Buchanan has organised to fly all of you to Los Angeles as a reward for Mr Bigsby's loyal service,' said Weaver.

'What about Archie?' asked Holly.

'He should go home to his mother,' said Big Hair.

'He can't,' said Mr Bigsby. 'His mother's been taken ill. We'll have to contact the local authorities.'

'That will take too much time,' said Weaver. 'Mr Buchanan is insistent that you come back with me immediately and that your family join you.'

'It's most kind of him,' said Big Hair.

'As you already know, Global Sands is a very generous employer,' said Weaver. 'If there is nowhere else for the boy to go, you can bring him with you.'

'But what about passports? What about parental permission? We're not the child's legal guardians,' squawked Big Hair.

'Passports are no problem,' said Weaver dismissively. 'And I shall see to it personally that there are no problems with taking the boy. Global Sands has a great deal of influence.' He looked Big Hair directly in the eyes. 'Alternatively you can stay to sort out the boy's welfare while your husband and daughter go ahead without you.'

'Of course Archie should come with us,' said Big Hair quick as a flash. 'He's almost one of the family now.'

Holly felt something rub against her leg. She picked up Willow. 'What about her?' she asked.

'I'll arrange for your neighbours to look after her

while you're away,' replied Weaver.

'Right, that's it settled, then,' said Mr Bigsby, clapping his hands together. 'We're going to America.'

With those words Holly and Archie felt all the awful reality of the evening disappear, lost beneath a wave of excitement.

'And you have ten minutes to pack your bags,' said Weaver.

Chapter Eight

Brant Buchanan stepped out of the car on to the wide San Franciscan road outside a laundrette.

'Long way to come to do your washing,' joked his temporary chauffeur.

Buchanan checked the address against the one Weaver had written down for him.

'Stay here,' he said, entering the building.

Inside, two large black ladies were folding sheets. They stopped as he entered and turned to look at him. In his designer clothes and expensive shoes, Brant Buchanan clearly wasn't their usual customer.

'Can I help you, honey?' one of them said.

'I'm looking for Frank Hunter,' he replied.

The women looked at each other then burst into hysterics. Brant Buchanan felt a rare sensation of discomfort.

'That's two people, sweetie, and they're through that door,' said the other.

'Thank you,' replied Mr Buchanan, walking the length of the laundrette and finding a door with a piece of paper pinned to it. It read:

Frank Hunter Inexplicable Investigations
Please knock before entering

Brant turned the handle.

'Aren't you going to knock?' asked the first lady.

'I'm expected,' he replied, stepping into a dark room and shutting the door behind him.

'Nooo!' cried a voice inside.

Outside the two ladies were hooting with laughter.

A light came on and a man with long black hair and a goatee beard stood in front of Brant, holding a blank piece of photographic paper and looking distraught.

'Man,' he moaned. 'Have you never heard of knocking?'

'I'm sorry, I understood you were expecting me.'

'Expecting you to come barging into my dark room

and ruin the picture I was developing? Why would I expect something like that, man?'

'My name is Brant –'

'And my name's Frank,' interrupted the man, 'but what's that got to do with this non-knocking policy of yours?'

'Frank, man, cool it, this is Brant Buchanan, the English dude I told you about,' said a second man, entering the room. This one had lighter hair and an under-chin beard. 'Pleased to meet you, Mr Buchanan, sir. Sorry about Frank. He gets tetchy. I'm Hunter. I'm the one who spoke to your colleague. I'm really pleased to meet you, man.' He extended his hand.

Brant Buchanan tentatively shook it. 'I'm sorry about your friend's picture. I didn't know anyone developed pictures these days. I thought it was all digital.'

Hunter laughed. 'Yeah, well, Frank likes to do things the old-fashioned way. I keep telling him to go digital.'

'Was the Loch Ness monster caught on digital? Were Big Foot or the Roswell alien on digital? No, man, none of them were,' said Frank, picking up a pile of photos from one of the messy workspaces that surrounded the room. He held out three blurry black and white pictures that Buchanan recognised as apparent sightings of unexplained things.

'That's because digital hadn't been invented then, man,' said Hunter.

'Or had it?'

'Not this again,' sighed Hunter.

'It's what I believe, man,' said Frank.

'Not in front of guests,' insisted Hunter. 'Remember, we have a rule.'

Frank hesitated.

'No, please, I'm an open-minded man,' said Buchanan. 'That is why I'm here after all. Say whatever you have to say.'

'See, *he's* open-minded, man,' said Frank.

Hunter sighed.

'I believe that digital photography was created in order to stop us from finding out the truth,' said Frank. 'Unlike old-fashioned technology it was created by – and is now being controlled by – super-intelligent aliens that live right here on earth with us, man.' He whispered this as though someone might be listening.

'And where are these aliens?' asked Mr Buchanan.

'They're all around us,' Frank whispered. 'They're cats, man. You should see the way they look at me. They know I know.'

'Frank, man,' interrupted Hunter, 'you sound crazy

when you talk like that.'

Brant Buchanan began to edge towards the door. 'I'm sorry, I think I've made a mistake.'

'No, man, don't go,' said Hunter. 'It's just Frank. He's perfectly fine except for the alien cats thing. You want to know about dragons, don't you?'

Buchanan paused. 'Do you know who I am?'

'Of course. You're Brant Buchanan, the seventh richest man in the world. You founded Global Sands, the most awesome multinational company in the universe, man.'

'This is Brant Buchanan?' said Frank. 'Why didn't you say so, Hunter?'

'I tried, man, but no, you had to tell him your whole cats-are-aliens thing. Man, you should keep that stuff for your film scripts.'

'Let me make myself clear,' said Mr Buchanan. 'I have recently become interested in dragons. I don't care about aliens or vampires or things that go bump in the night. I'm not interested in any conspiracy theories on how the government covers things up because, believe me, no government in the world has any secrets from me, but a man in my position can't afford to let anyone find out that I'm in business with gentlemen such as yourselves. My stock would plummet. We live in a world of non-believers, my friends. People would think I had gone mad if they thought I believed in dragons. Help me gather information discreetly and you will be handsomely rewarded.'

Frank put the photos down. 'Yeah, well, I could be wrong about the cats, I suppose,' he said.

'You want stuff on dragons?' said Hunter.

'Yes, I want stuff on dragons,' replied Buchanan.

Chapter Nine

For Holly and Archie it didn't seem quite real. Weaver had driven them to Heathrow Airport, where, without delays or queues, they boarded a luxury private jet, which took them to America.

After take-off, Holly and Archie spent the first couple of hours running around the plane, looking at all the cool stuff. When Holly's dad told them to sit still, they played computer games then decided to watch a film.

'I could get used to this,' said Archie.

'It certainly beats being stuck inside that house,' said Holly, lying back in her comfy bed, with her head on the soft pillow. The film was one she had really wanted to see but she only managed to watch the opening credits before her exhaustion caught up with her and she was asleep.

When she awoke, the captain was announcing that they would be landing shortly in Los Angeles, where the local time would be 5 a.m.

'If you look over to your right, you can see the deserts of California,' he added.

Holly looked out of the window sleepily. The sun was rising in the sky, reddening the barren landscape. She thought about Dirk. She would phone him when they arrived and tell him where she was.

When the plane landed, there was no messing about with customs or passports. They simply went straight through to the car park, where a black stretch limo was awaiting them.

'You'll be staying in the Hollywood Hills,' said Weaver.

'Where they make all the films?' said Holly.

'You won't be far from the major studios,' he replied matter-of-factly.

Big Hair could barely contain herself.

'Wow, this is real star treatment,' she squealed.

The limo took them to the city. Seeing a street sign saying 'Hollywood', Holly was surprised to see that, in spite of the palm trees that lined the roads, the area actually looked quite ordinary and grubby.

'Hey, you're Holly in Hollywood,' said Archie.

Then they headed up a winding road and the houses got bigger and more how Holly had imagined Hollywood would look. They came to a set of gates, which opened automatically. At the end of the driveway was a large white house with columns along the front and an upstairs balcony.

'This is where you'll be staying during your time here,' said Weaver.

When the car stopped, Holly and Archie burst out and ran to the house. It looked like part of a film set – too new and clean-looking to be a real house. Weaver opened the door. Inside, a central staircase led to a landing and four large rooms, all of which had doors that opened on to the balcony.

Archie pushed one wide open and stepped out. The vast city was laid out before them, bathed in the soft early morning light.

'Nice view,' he said.

'Try this one,' replied Holly. She was standing at the corner of the building looking the other way, up the hill. Archie joined her and saw what she was looking at.

Above them were nine giant letters set in the hills that spelt HOLLYWOOD.

'I imagine this sort of thing happens to you all the time,' said Archie.

'Oh, every day,' replied Holly.

'I may have to call my agent about my latest role,' said Archie.

'Me too. I need a much bigger part,' said Holly.

'Hey, I wonder if we're next door to anyone famous.'

They tried to see into next door's garden but the houses were designed so you couldn't see in from the balcony. Archie suggested they try looking from one of the trees next to the fence.

As they ran downstairs into the garden, they passed Big Hair who shouted, 'Stop running around, this isn't a playground.' Ignoring her, Holly and Archie found a climbable tree in the garden, and went up.

Next door looked more like a fairytale castle than a house. It had cherub-like gargoyles and turrets and it was painted bright pink. The patio door was open and a girl's voice cut through the air.

'I don't care what anyone else says,' said the girl. 'My mum's exec-producing this film and she agrees with me. We need to reshoot the birth scene with me playing myself . . .'

'Who do you think it is?' whispered Archie.

Holly knew exactly who it was. The patio door opened and Petal Moses stepped out. She was sporting a pink tracksuit and holding a phone to her ear.

'. . . Yes, I realise I would have been a baby, but I'm not having some other actor, baby or not, stealing my first scene . . . I'll be playing myself . . . Of course I know I don't look like a baby . . .' she yelled. 'That's why they call it acting, darling. Besides, Mum there's new technology where they can make me look like a baby if necessary . . . Chase says it's fine . . . Chase Lampton, the director, sweetie . . . Look, just drop the baby and let me know when I'm needed for the scene. OK?'

She switched off the phone and shook her head in frustration. 'Casting directors,' she exclaimed. 'What a nightmare.'

'Morning, Petal,' called Holly cheerfully.

Petal turned to see Holly halfway up the tree.

'You!' she said. 'What are you doing here, spying on me? I could have you arrested for invading my privacy.'

'We're neighbours. This is Archie.'

'Hello,' said Archie, waving.

'What are *you* doing in LA?' asked Petal sharply.

'My dad's working here,' said Holly.

'I see. Well, I'm making a film,' said Petal, smiling smugly. 'It's based on my book but we've made a few changes – you know, brought it up to date. It's still all about me, of course.'

'Is it a comedy?' asked Archie.

'No,' replied Petal. 'It's a heart-warming tale of one very special girl's struggle to grow up under the harsh media spotlight.'

'Sounds like a horror,' said Holly.

'You don't know anything about movies. Chase says I've really got something.'

'As long as you don't give it to us,' said Holly.

Before Petal could think of a retort a woman's voice called, 'Petal Moses, come and have some breakfast before piano practice. And I don't want to hear any more excuses about learning lines. I promised your mother I would make you musical, which is proving to be more difficult than trying to teach algebra to an orang-utan.'

'Miss Gilfeather?' said Holly in amazement.

The severe-looking music teacher from William Scrivener's School stepped out on to the patio holding a bowl of fruit and a glass of juice. Her auburn hair was hidden under a green beret. In spite of the strict tone she had taken with Petal she seemed more relaxed than when Holly had known her at school. Following Petal's gaze, she looked up at the tree and saw Holly and Archie.

'Holly Bigsby, third trumpet,' she said. 'I hope you're still practising every day.'

'Yes, Miss Gilfeather,' lied Holly, who hadn't picked up her trumpet for weeks.

'Such a shame you had to leave us,' said Miss Gilfeather warmly. 'You did show a little potential, unlike some students.' She looked at Petal.

'How dare you!' exclaimed Petal. 'Employing you was the biggest mistake my mother ever made. As soon as she gets out of the studio, I'll make sure she fires you.'

'Your mother employed me because she disagrees with me regarding your utter inability in the realms of music. She wants you to have the opportunity that she never had, to learn properly how to play an instrument.'

'Have you been here all summer?' asked Holly in disbelief, remembering how much disdain Miss Gilfeather had always showed for both Petal and her popstar mother.

Miss Gilfeather looked uncomfortable. 'Well, yes . . . I did have some misgivings when she asked but opportunities like this don't come along every day. I'd never been to this side of America before and I have to admit that pop stars pay rather better than schools . . .'

Petal's phone rang. 'Excuse me. Chase Lampton, the famous director, is calling me.' She walked back into the house and answered it. 'Oh, Chase, darling, are you coming round?'

'Why don't you join us for breakfast?' said Miss Gilfeather. 'There's plenty of food and I could do with some civilised conversation for a change.'

'Is that OK? And Archie too?' said Holly, who could hear Petal twittering on inside the house.

'Oh yes,' said Miss Gilfeather. 'As much as it annoys Madam, her mother put me in charge of the house while she's away recording her new album. Come round now and I'll make some pancakes.'

Chapter Ten

'Where are you going?' demanded Big Hair, as Holly and Archie made for the front door.

'We've been invited next door for breakfast. Miss Gilfeather is staying there.'

'Your old music teacher?' said Big Hair. 'What a small world it is. I wouldn't want to decorate it though,' she added, laughing at her own joke.

Archie and Holly looked at each other. America appeared to have had a rather odd effect on Big Hair.

'So it's OK to go round?' said Holly.

'Of course. Don't be too long, I thought we'd go and see the sights later on,' she said.

Holly and Archie headed down the drive.

'I think the sun's gone to her head,' said Archie, looking up at the perfect blue sky.

'Don't knock it,' said Holly.

She pressed the buzzer outside Petal's house and the gate opened. They headed up the driveway and Miss Gilfeather welcomed them into the house. The walls were covered with framed discs, album artwork and photos from Petal's mum's career. A cabinet by the door displayed hundreds of gleaming awards in different shapes and sizes. In the centre of the hallway, at the base of the sweeping staircase, was a life-sized marble statue of Petal's mother kneeling in what looked like a puddle. Water trickled down from the statue's eyes and at the base of the statue was a gold plaque that read: 'She weeps for world peace'.

'Apparently it's the name of one of her albums,' said Miss Gilfeather. 'Isn't it hideous?'

The buzzer sounded and Petal appeared at the top of the stairs.

'Will you get that, Miss Gilfeather? It'll be Chase . . .' She stopped, noticing Holly and Archie. 'What are you doing here?'

'I invited them round, and I am not your servant, Petal,' said Miss Gilfeather, pressing the button to open the gate.

'You can't go inviting people round my house.'

'As you well know, I am in charge in your mother's absence,' said Miss Gilfeather. 'Holly did, at least, show some glimmer of natural ability at the trumpet. Do you play anything?' she asked Archie.

'My dad gave me a guitar once,' replied Archie.

'A lovely instrument if played well,' said Miss Gilfeather approvingly.

'Only the strings hurt my fingers and then he flogged it,' he added.

'Learning any instrument always involves an element of pain to begin with,' said the music teacher. 'More often for those having to listen to the beginner's efforts, but one must go through the pain barrier in order to achieve beauty.'

'Then what pain did you go through to achieve such captivating charm?' said a man, entering the hallway. He had thick curly black hair and was wearing an expensive pair of sunglasses.

'Good morning, Mr Lampton,' said Miss Gilfeather. 'Is it too bright for you in here?'

The man smiled and removed his sunglasses to reveal dark brown eyes. 'Hi, Vivian,' he replied in a cool American accent. 'And, please, it's Chase to my friends.'

'Until we become friends I will stick with Mr Lampton, Mr Lampton. I'll make some coffee,' replied Miss Gilfeather, walking to the kitchen.

'Hi, Chase,' beamed Petal, suddenly developing an American twang in her voice.

'And how is my talented leading lady?'

'I'm fine, thanks, Chase. Where's Dante?'

'He's on the phone to his agent. He'll be in in a minute. I see you've got guests this morning,' said Chase, nodding at Holly and Archie. 'I hope you two aren't distracting our star here.'

'Oh, just ignore them,' said Petal. 'They aren't anybody.'

'That's right, we're nobody,' said Holly.

'I used to be somebody, but now I'm not anybody,' said Archie.

Chase smiled and said to Petal, 'Did you manage to get a chance to look through the rewrite for the final scene?'

'Yes, I've made a few notes. I was thinking what if . . . wait for it . . .what if I were to fly at the end of the film?'

'Fly?' said Chase.

'Yes, what do you think? Mum thinks it would be a great way to end the film.'

Chase paused as if visualising the idea, then nodded. 'Yeah, I can see that working. You could fly right over all the teachers and pupils in the concert. Real feel-good moment. Great idea.'

'It ends with a concert?' said Holly.

'That's right,' said Chase, 'Petal's big moment when she sang her first solo at the school concert this year. It's not in the book but we thought it would make a good ending for the movie. We're filming it today. Why don't you come down and sit in the audience? It would be good to get some genuine Brit accents.'

'I think you'll find mine to be a genuine British accent, Papa,' said a boy who entered behind Chase, with the same thick black hair, sunglasses, leather jacket and designer jeans as the director.

'Hi, Dante,' said Petal.

'Good morning, Petal,' said Dante in an English accent that caused Holly and Archie to fall about laughing. 'What's so funny?' he asked, reverting to his normal American voice.

'Nothing,' said Archie, controlling himself. 'I thought it was a splendid accent, old bean.'

'Hey, thanks,' said Dante. 'I'm Dante Lampton. I play Callum Thackley, the disturbed but musically brilliant son of the Prime Minister.'

'He's not that musically brilliant,' said Petal.

'Callum's in the film?' said Holly, astonished.

'It's only a supporting role,' said Petal.

'I wanted to use the character of Callum to show how people deal with things differently,' said Chase Lampton.

'Callum's not a character. He's a real person,' said Holly.

'What interests me is how the same kind of media attention that Petal thrives on is what drove poor Callum mad,' said Chase.

'That's not fair . . .' said Holly, but she could hardly explain how the monsters that haunted Callum were not figments of his imagination but very real dragons.

'Oh yes, I forgot Holly had a crush on Callum,' said Petal.

'I did not,' said Holly. 'We just played in the band together.'

'So you were at the concert too?' said Chase. 'Tell me what you can remember about it. We're recreating it today but there's no footage of it.'

Holly could remember every detail of the horrific night when the Dark Mountain Dragon, Vainclaw Grandin, had entranced the hall with Dragonsong but she lied and said, 'I only remember how good it was.'

'Ha! You see,' said Chase, snapping his fingers, 'that's what everyone says. It's kind of spooky. You know, there are rumours on the Internet that something strange happened that night – like something, you know, magic.'

'What nonsense. Unless you are referring to the magic of music,' said Miss Gilfeather, stepping into the hallway, not realising how close to the truth she was. After all, it was Dirk's Dragonsong which had caused everyone to forget the evening.

Chase smiled. 'You know, Vivian, it's not too late to play yourself. The actress playing you isn't a patch on the real thing.'

'I'm sure she would be flattered to hear you say so,' replied Miss Gilfeather. 'I'll be quite content as a member of the audience.'

'Can we sit with you?' said Holly.

'Of course,' said Miss Gilfeather. 'Now come along. Breakfast is ready in the dining room.'

The buzzer sounded.

'You go ahead,' said Chase. 'That'll be Theo. He's all wound up about something as usual. You go through. I'll be there in a minute.'

'Theo is Chase's assistant director,' explained Miss

75

Gilfeather, leading them into the dining room.

'So do you want to be an actor when you grow up?' Holly said to Dante.

'I'm an actor now,' he replied. 'I'm going to be a director when I grow up like Dad. Acting is a good way to get to know the business. Do you want to be in the movies too?'

'No, I'm going to be a detective,' replied Holly, picturing herself sitting in an office like Dirk's or wearing a wide-brimmed hat like Ladbroke Blake, another detective she knew who had once been hired to follow her and had, ever since, helped her out of some tight spots.

'Since you know Callum, can you tell me what you think of my impression?' said Dante. 'I want to get him just right but I've not been allowed to meet him.'

Dante turned round and tried to flatten his unkempt hair against his head. When he turned to face them again, he had a strange look on his face and he allowed his eyes to roll around in his head. Holly had to admit that it wasn't a bad likeness of Callum. Dante walked around the dining-room table, allowing his right leg to drag behind him in a limp and spoke in his attempt at an English accent. 'My name is Callum Thackley. They call me Crazy Callum. But it is not I who is mad. It is you.' Dante relaxed, smiled, and said in his normal voice, 'What do you think?'

'Well . . . It's not bad,' said Holly, 'but Callum doesn't really have a limp.'

'I know that,' replied Dante, with a theatrical wave of his hand, 'but I thought it would help bring the character alive.'

'Yes, but he doesn't have one,' said Holly.

'I like the limp,' said Petal.

'Oh, it's a good limp,' said Holly, catching Archie's eye.

'An excellent limp,' said Archie.

'If I hadn't known, I'd have thought you were actually lame,' said Holly.

'Totally lame,' added Archie, straight-faced.

'Thanks,' replied Dante. 'Hey, I like these guys, Petal.'

They sat down at the table and helped themselves to the breakfast Miss Gilfeather had laid out.

In the hallway they could hear someone talking loudly.

'Chase, I don't know where to start . . . The whole thing's crazy . . .' he was saying.

'Calm down, Theo,' said Chase. 'Let's go and get something to eat. I need a coffee.' He led a fair-haired, red-faced man into the room. The man was breathing heavily and flapping his arms agitatedly. Chase poured himself a coffee and sat down. 'Now what is it?' he said.

The other man remained standing, continually moving with nervous energy. He took a deep breath then spoke. 'We were filming in the desert . . .'

'Why do we need a boring old desert in the film?' asked Petal.

'It's for the opening sequence. It's symbolic, you know, representing a cultural desert, isolation . . . that kind of thing,' said Chase.

'Yeah, well, we got lots of nice shots using the long-angle lens . . .' continued Theo. 'We went early morning and just where you said, two miles down the road from the southern entrance to Joshua Tree National Park. You were right, the light's real nice at dusk. It made for real pretty shots. The sun was coming up and the desert had a kind of reddish glow.'

'Sounds beautiful,' said Chase, stirring cream into his coffee.

'Then . . .' Theo faltered. 'Then something got in the way of the shot.'

'What sort of something?'

'Something big. It was in the distance but you could see what it was. There were two of them. I looked

78

back at the film to check.'

'Well,' said Chase patiently, 'what was it? A road-runner? A wolf? There's not much that lives out there.'

'It wasn't any of those things,' said Theo. 'It was . . . Well, it looked like . . . You know, from a distance it seemed to be . . .'

'Spit it out,' said Chase. 'I haven't got all day.'

'D . . . d . . . d . . . dragons,' whispered the red-faced man.

Petal and Dante hooted with laughter.

A smile spread across Chase's face.

Holly and Archie said nothing.

'I think you may have got the wrong idea about the sort of movie we're making,' said Chase, sipping his coffee.

'Look, I know it sounds crazy but I know what I saw and I saw dragons. They looked like those Joshua trees you get out there – you know, all spiky like cactuses, but they had jaws and limbs and they were fighting.'

'How ridiculous,' said Petal scornfully. 'Dragons don't exist in real life, do they, Chase?'

'Not in my experience,' replied the director ponder-ously. 'Look, Theo, I'll tell you what, let me see the rushes. I'd like to have a look at these dragons. It's probably just a trick of the light.'

'That's the problem,' said Theo. 'That's what's so odd. Everyone will think I'm making it up but I know what I saw.'

'Then let me see the film,' said Chase firmly.

'I can't,' replied Theo. 'The film's gone missing. It was stolen.'

Chapter Eleven

Dirk was in the middle of a dream about the moon being a huge orange, which had ripened and was heading on a collision course with earth, when the phone rang.

'Someone get a juicer!' cried Dirk, waking up with a start. His mouth was parched and two empty bottles of orange squash lay on his desk. He groaned, knocked them on to the floor, and answered the ringing phone.

'The Dragon Detective Agency,' he said gruffly. 'Dirk Dilly speaking. How can I help you?'

'Have you just woken up?' It was Holly. 'What time is it there?'

'What do you mean *there*? Where are you?' said Dirk.

'I'm calling long distance,' said Holly. 'I'm in Los Angeles.'

'Los Angeles in America?' spluttered Dirk.

'No, Los Angeles in Kuala Lumpur,' said Holly, laughing.

'I thought you were grounded,' said Dirk.

'We got flown here on Brant Buchanan's private jet.'

'I don't trust your dad's boss as far as I can throw him. In fact, I don't trust him as far as he can throw me.'

'Nor do I, but that's not why I'm calling. Have you ever heard of Chase Lampton?'

'The film director? Yes,' said Dirk. 'He directed one of my favourite films, *The Big Zero*. He never made anything as good since, but that one was a classic.'

'Well, he's making a new film now, only one of the cameras caught something in the desert first thing this morning.'

'What kind of something?'

'Dragons,' said Holly.

'Rats in pyjamas!' exclaimed Dirk, sitting up. 'This is serious. Where's the film?'

'No one knows. It's been stolen.'

'You were right to call. We can't let that film stay in human hands,' said Dirk. 'The way things work these days that evidence could be all over the Internet by lunchtime. Then it's game over.'

Dirk took down the phone number and address of where Holly was staying and committed them both to memory. Holly said what she knew about where the film had been made and then she told him about their amazing journey to America and how Chase had asked her and Archie to be in the film too.

After saying goodbye Dirk put down the receiver, opened a desk drawer and pulled out Mrs Klingerflim's copy of *Dragonlore*, flicking to the chapter on Desert Dragons.

The Desert Dragon is different from other subspecies of dragon in that it spits a deadly poison rather than breathing fire. The poison is a potent acid that will cut through the strongest material, fell a mighty tree or kill any creature in seconds. However, Desert Dragons can only hold one dose of poison at a time, which takes them around twenty-four hours to produce. So once the poison is used up all you have to worry about are the teeth, claws and hundreds of spikes which cover their bodies.

Dirk placed the book back in the drawer and considered the best way to get to America. Flying, swimming or taking the lithosphere tunnel would take too long. If there was a possibility that the film was being watched by a human, he had to move fast. Dirk switched off the TV and headed downstairs.

He stopped outside the kitchen, where Mrs Klingerflim was clattering about preparing her dinner, humming along to some old crackly jazz that was coming from her tinny radio. She held down a button on top of her oven, creating the hiss of gas and a clicking noise, but failing to light the hob.

'Bother to this old thing!' she exclaimed. 'Oh, Mr Dilly, excuse my language. I didn't see you there.'

'Let me help you with that,' said Dirk.

She stood back. Dirk leant over the hob and sent a tiny flicker of flame from between his two front teeth, lighting it. Mrs Klingerflim smiled and placed a pan of water on it.

'Thank you, Mr Dilly,' she said. 'Off out, are you?'

'I've got a case out of town so I wanted to let you know that the rent may be a little late and that I won't be around to help.'

'Oh, don't worry about that,' said the sweet old lady. 'I've always got Mr Blandford. He pops round sometimes to help out. He put up these shelves.'

'Sounds like you've got an admirer,' said Dirk, winking.

'Oh, Mr Dilly, don't be daft,' said Mrs Klingerflim, blushing and changing the subject. 'Are you going anywhere nice?'

'California,' replied Dirk.

Mrs Klingerflim smiled wistfully. 'California. How lovely. I went there with Ivor once, you know. Stunning scenery.'

'Dragon-spotting?' asked Dirk. All of Mrs Klingerflim's holidays with her late husband, Ivor, had been research for the book.

'Oh yes, those Californian Desert Dragons are very territorial but beautiful movers. I wouldn't want to get on the wrong side of one, mind.'

'I'll bear that in mind,' he said. 'No skydiving while I'm away, Mrs K.'

'Oh, I'll be too busy wrestling crocodiles,' said the frail old lady. 'How are you getting there?'

'Smelding,' replied Dirk.

'Oh, really? How interesting. Good luck.'

Dirk left her and went down to the cellar, climbing into the hole Karnataka had made and clawing his way through the broken bits of concrete into the ground.

Soon he reached the rock that lay beneath the foundations of the house.

In the dark Dirk lay flat on the rock and concentrated on relaxing every muscle in his body. It wasn't easy but after a few seconds he felt a tingling pain on the soft skin of his belly and the underside of his neck and limbs.

In his book, Ivor Klingerflim described smelding like this:

The act of smelding is unique to Mountain Dragons and is an extension of blending. Only, rather than repositioning particles that form the colour of a surface over the dragon, it involves the dragon squeezing each particle of his body between the particles that form the rock beneath him. The process of reducing itself to formless particles takes the dragon around an hour but it means there is no resistance and that he can choose to re-emerge anywhere in the world.

Dirk wasn't sure about the science of it but he did know that it hurt. The knack with smelding was to stay relaxed during the extremely painful process, which felt like being eaten by a million tiny sharp-toothed fish. It was a technique developed during the

Ice Age, when dragons had to travel thousands of miles to find edible vegetation. Dirk was grateful that he lived in more convenient times. It was bad enough when his supermarket got his order wrong and sent him the cheap tins of beans that were all sauce and no beans.

Eventually he felt himself smelding into the rock, his skin, bones and green blood slipping into the spaces in between the particles. Once fully immersed, it was an odd feeling. Without eyes he couldn't see anything, and without paws he couldn't feel anything. He knew he still existed but, without a physical body, there was an extreme lightness to his existence that was ultimately very relaxing. He had heard of dragons who had never reappeared after having smelded and Dirk could understand why. He fought the lethargy that had swept over him and sensed a rock in the Californian Desert where he could begin the equally painful re-emergence.

By the time he felt sunlight on his face Dirk was exhausted. He looked weakly at the scenery in front of his newly formed eyes. A dusty, stony landscape stretched out in front of him as far as he could see. Strange leafless trees with twisted branches were dotted around, each growing a metre or so apart. The thick branches were covered in light brown spikes with clumps of green spikes at the end. Dirk recognised them as Joshua trees from a nature programme he had seen once. Between them dry shrubs struggled to find enough water to survive. All around were huge piles of boulders and rocks, like the one where Dirk was emerging. The sky was pastel blue with only a couple of fluffy clouds to accompany the blazing sun. There wasn't a living creature in sight.

The final piece of Dirk's claws appeared and he collapsed and passed out from exhaustion.

When he awoke, the sun was high in the sky and every part of his body ached. Vowing to take a slower but easier route home he stretched, jumped down from the rock and began searching for any signs of dragons. He checked the more healthy shrubs, looking for nibble marks. He examined the ground for footprints. The problem with tracking dragons was that, unlike humans, they left very little indication of where they had been.

Dirk heard a noise. He stopped dead. Something had moved but all he could see were the strangely shaped Joshua trees. It was probably a desert rat or a wolf but as a precaution he raised himself on to his hind legs and drew his claws, prepared to fight if necessary.

He remained perfectly still, listening for another sound. He turned round as something flew over him. A weight landed on his back. He stumbled forward, tripped on a root and fell to the ground. Spikes dug into his skin, so sharp he could even feel them through the hard skin on his back. Dirk craned his neck around just enough to catch a glimpse of the spiky face of a particularly vicious-looking Desert Dragon before it pushed his head to the ground. Strong limbs pinned him to the floor and a thin voice said, 'You looking to rumble, dragon? You come trespassin' on my turf lookin' for a fight?'

Chapter Twelve

'I surrender,' said Dirk, hoping that the Desert Dragon on his back had already used up his day's worth of poison.

'That's real funny,' said an incredulous voice. 'You come struttin' into my territory, ready to rumble, and you expect me to believe that you surrender? Old Putz ain't no klutz. You're a friend of Kitelsky's, ain't you? I shoulda saw it comin', a cheap trick like this. He don't wanna play fair no more.'

'Listen, Putz, my name's Dirk Dilly. I'm a detective. I didn't come here to fight and I don't know anyone called Kitelsky,' said Dirk.

'Dirk Dilly? What kind of silly name is that?'

'It's my name,' snarled Dirk, 'and don't call me silly.'

'You don't get to give orders on my turf, OK, particularly when I found you with your claws ready flicked,' said Putz.

'I only drew my claws because I heard a noise,' said Dirk.

'A noise? I didn't make no noise. Old Putz is a silent assailant.'

'Sure you made a noise,' said another voice.

'Kitelsky,' growled Putz. 'I knew it. So he is with you.'

At first it looked to Dirk like one of the Joshua trees was moving, but what Dirk had taken for branches were thick limbs. What had looked like a mound of dead grass at the foot of the tree was a dragon's head at the end of a long neck, with two yellow eyes set in the middle. A tail swung into view, with a cone of white spikes at the end.

'He ain't wi' me,' said Kitelsky. 'It looks to me like he's wi' you.'

'If he were wi' me, why would I be pinning him down, which I am doing, I should say, with no small degree of ease and expertise?' replied Putz.

'Because that's how you treat your friends, Putz,' replied Kitelsky bitterly.

Dirk felt the weight lift from his back as Putz flew at Kitelsky, his spikes splayed out, but Kitelsky was ready for him, diving out of the way, leaving Putz to land into a roll before jumping back on to all fours and squaring off.

Putz's skin was lighter than Kitelsky's, with sharp green spikes on the end of his tail, and, where Kitelsky had a grassy beard, Putz's craggy chin was visible. He snarled, showing his white teeth.

Maintaining eye contact, the two dragons started to sidestep, head to head, moving in a circle. A bubbling noise came from the backs of their throats. Dirk edged away.

As they paced, he understood what Mrs Klingerflim had meant about their movements being beautiful. They stepped in perfect time with each other. It was like watching a graceful dance.

Then Putz broke step. He opened his mouth wide and spat a stream of luminous green liquid at the other dragon. Kitelsky ducked and the liquid flew over his head, hitting the tree behind him, which hissed as the poison burnt straight through its bark and caused it to fall to the ground.

Neither Desert Dragon looked at the tree, their yellow eyes remaining fixed on each other as they moved back and forth. Without warning Kitelsky took a side-step then spat poison at Putz. Putz jumped into the air to avoid it, somersaulting over Kitelsky, who spun round, bringing them face to face again.

'You're trespassin' on my turf,' said Putz.

'This ain't your territory and you know it,' replied Kitelsky.

'I'm claimin' it,' said Putz.

'You gotta earn it first.'

'Let's rumble, then.'

The two dragons went at each other with claws, teeth and spikes. As vicious as it looked, it seemed to Dirk that they knew each other's moves so well that they barely made contact. It looked more like an elaborate routine than a real fight.

After a while the two dragons began to tire.

'Your Mountain Dragon ain't gettin' involved, then,' said Putz, standing back.

'I told you, he ain't wi' me,' replied Kitelsky.

'Well, he ain't wi' me either,' said Putz.

They both turned to look at Dirk.

'You only get one dose of poison a day,' said Dirk, who had been ready for this. 'I get fire 24-7.'

He sent flames billowing forward, setting the fallen branch on fire. The Desert Dragons stepped back from the burning tree.

'You fire dragons are all the same,' said Putz. 'You think you're so much better than us. It still don't change the fact that you're trespassin' on my turf.'

'Putz, this is Mo's turf,' said Kitelsky. 'And you're only jealous. Putz is always trying to breathe fire.'

'No I ain't,' said Putz.

'You're pathetic,' said Kitelsky.

'Are there any other dragons in the area?' asked Dirk.

'Not since Mo left, no,' said Kitelsky. 'Just us two. Why?'

'Where were you at dawn this morning?' asked Dirk.

'We were scufflin',' said Kitelsky.

'What's that mean?'

'It's when you fight for your territory,' said Putz. 'You beat a dragon in a scuffle and you got their turf. We do it at sunrise and sunset on the borders of our territory.'

'Yeah, and you never beaten Mo, so this ain't your turf,' said Kitelsky.

'Only cos he ain't here to scuffle wi' me,' said Putz, squaring up for another fight.

'I'm not interested in your territorial disputes,' said

Dirk, sending another blast of fire into the air as a warning.

'What do you want, then?' said Kitelsky.

'Two dragons were caught on film this morning,' said Dirk. 'You know what film is, I take it?'

'Of course we do,' said Kitelsky. 'You can't live in California without knowing what film is.'

'That's right,' said Putz. 'We ain't stupid.'

'Then you'll know that the punishment for being seen by a human is banishment to the Inner Core,' said Dirk.

'The Inner Core?' said Putz, the colour draining from his face.

'What's it to you, anyway, Dilly?' said Kitelsky. 'You come here saying we done this and that. We don't even know you.'

'You know what?' snapped Dirk angrily. 'You're right, I should leave you to it. I was going to find and destroy the tape but now I might just go home and crack open a fresh bottle of squash in front of a good movie instead.'

'Hey, don't be so hasty,' said Putz. 'Kitelsky don't mean to disrespect you or nuttin'. Do you, Kitelsky?'

'I don't trust him,' said Kitelsky. 'How do we know he ain't gonna do the dirty on us?'

'I haven't got time for this. I'm going to retrieve that tape and save your spiky necks,' said Dirk, turning to leave. He could tell that the Desert Dragons didn't know any more than they were letting on. He was wasting his time.

'Where you going?' said Kitelsky.

'Los Angeles,' replied Dirk.

'We're comin' wi' you,' said Kitelsky.

'Are you outa your mind, Kitelsky?' said Putz. 'I ain't going to no human city.'

'You stay here, then,' replied Kitelsky. 'I don't trust this Mountain Dragon.'

'I work alone,' said Dirk.

'Did I say I was givin' you the choice?' said Kitelsky. 'If there's a film showin' me and Putz, I ain't gonna sit around and leave it to no out-of-town detective to sort out.'

'I'm goin' if you're goin',' said Putz.

'And what do you know about city life?' said Dirk.

'That ain't the point. Like it or not, we're comin' wi' you,' said Kitelsky.

Chapter Thirteen

'This is weird,' said Archie, reaching into his pocket and pulling out a jelly bean.

'It's really weird,' agreed Holly.

They were sitting on wooden chairs in the front row of an exact replica of Little Hope Village Hall where Holly's school concert had taken place. The fake hall was perfect down to the finest detail, except for one of the walls being missing, revealing that they were actually inside a huge hangar in the World Studios. Where the wall should have been were cameras and hundreds of people who bustled around with clipboards and expensive-looking equipment. Chase Lampton sat in a director's chair wearing a pair of sunglasses and a look of frustration.

During the eleven takes so far Petal hadn't even come close to remembering the words to the dreary song her mother had written for the grand finale of the film.

To keep everyone occupied between takes Theo Leggett was telling the band members their character names in case it helped them get into their parts.

Holly, Archie and Miss Gilfeather were in the audience, so they didn't have character names.

'On third trumpet we have Holly Bigsby,' said Theo, pointing at a blonde girl with exceptionally white teeth.

'Excellent likeness,' said Miss Gilfeather under her breath.

'So is yours,' said Holly, pointing to the stick-thin, beautiful young actress who was playing Miss Gilfeather and waving a baton around.

'What does that woman think she's doing?' said Miss Gilfeather.

'Looks like she's sword-fighting the Invisible Man,' said Archie.

Miss Gilfeather allowed herself a tiny smile. 'It's certainly not conducting,' she said. 'That emaciated young lady couldn't conduct a survey on whether monkeys like bananas. And as for that Lampton boy, he looks like he's never seen a French horn before.'

Dante Lampton was sitting at the front of the stage, in character as Callum Thackley, holding the instrument upside down.

'OK, everybody.' Chase spoke through a loudhailer. 'We're ready for another take. Petal Moses to set, please.'

Petal Moses arrived in one of the little white buggies used to shuttle the more important cast members to and from the VIP area. She got out of the buggy and drifted on to the set, wearing an extremely sparkly dress. She took her place in front of the stage, took a deep breath and said, 'I'm ready.'

'Quiet on set, please. *Petal – The Movie*, scene fifty-six, take twelve,' shouted a man with a clapperboard.

The lights dimmed and the music began.

'Excellent, I love this tune,' said Archie, forcing Holly to stifle her giggles.

'Don't make me laugh,' she said. 'I need the loo.'

'I bet you a jelly bean she messes up again,' whispered Archie.

'Be quiet,' scolded Miss Gilfeather. 'We'll only have to hear it again.'

'All she has to do is mime along with herself. How difficult can it be?' said Holly, under her breath.

As if in answer to her question, Chase shouted, 'Cut!'

'Anything wrong, Chase, darling?' asked Petal sweetly.

'Petal, love, remember what we said about moving your mouth in time with the words,' replied the director.

'I'm sorry, Chase. I keep forgetting where I come in.'

'You've got four bars, then the twiddly piano bit, then you come in,' said Chase.

'Oh yes. Sorry, Chase.'

'That's fine,' said Chase patiently.

'Dad, can I ask something?' said Dante.

'Sure thing, son,' replied Chase.

'I was thinking that my character would be fairly conflicted here, you know, pleased that he is in the concert but bitter that Petal's getting the limelight, like both happy and unhappy at the same time. Like this.'

Dante pulled a face.

'He looks more like he's both constipated and got diarrhoea at the same time,' said Archie.

Holly shook with laughter. 'Stop it! I really need the toilet,' she said.

'That's perfect, son,' said Chase. 'OK, let's take a fifteen-minute break, then we'll go for it one more time.'

'Great! I'm going to the toilet,' said Holly.

'I'd hurry. I don't think you're the only one with that idea,' said Miss Gilfeather, pointing at the swarm of people heading in the same direction. Holly and Archie tried to get through, but the crowd was bottle-necking at the door by the stage.

'Let's try a short cut,' said Archie, walking around the side of the wall.

Holly's heart sank when she saw that there was already a long queue coming from the girls' toilets.

'I'm bursting,' she moaned.

'Hi, guys,' said Dante as he passed them on one of the electric buggies, sitting next to his dad.

'I bet they don't have to queue for the toilet,' said Archie.

'I know, but you need one of those passes,' replied Holly, watching as the buggy reached a doorway and a security guard checked their passes and waved them through.

'If only you could turn invisible,' said Archie, with a

wide grin. 'Oh, hold on . . . You can.'

Holly smiled then said, 'What about you?'

'I'll be fine – the queue isn't as long for the boys. I'll cause a diversion. Look, there's Theo.' Theo Leggett was driving a buggy towards the exit. Archie ran over to him. 'Excuse me, Mr Leggett,' he said.

Theo slammed his foot on the brake. 'Hey, be careful,' he said.

'Sorry, Mr Leggett, sir, but I've been meaning to ask how you get to become an assistant director.'

Theo beamed at Archie. 'The first thing you need is a love of film,' he said, sounding like he had been waiting all his life for someone to ask this. 'From a very young age I've always loved movies. But that's not enough. You have to be willing to work hard. The hours are long but in the end . . .'

While he spoke, Holly sneaked round the back of the buggy, checked no one was looking and climbed on. Theo must have caught a glimpse of her in the corner of his eye because he broke off what he was saying to glance back, but Holly had vanished. He turned back to Archie.

'I need to get going,' he said. 'Here, take my card. When you're old enough, give me a call. Maybe I can give you your first break.'

'That's great,' said Archie, putting the card into his back pocket. 'Thanks for the advice.'

'No problem. Keep your dreams alive,' said Theo, driving the buggy towards the door, past the guard, out of the building, briefly into the bright sunshine, and across the tarmac to another hangar, where there were a few office desks, a coffee bar and, Holly was pleased to notice, a row of toilets with no queue.

Theo parked the buggy and went to get a coffee. Holly checked no one was looking and ran to the toilet

With her bladder finally relieved she went back to Theo's buggy, climbed on and blended into the seat, waiting for Theo to take her back.

She had been waiting for a minute, watching Theo attempt to drink his coffee without getting his nose covered in froth, when she saw Chase and Dante Lampton walking over to where she was hiding. Chase had an arm around Dante's shoulders. For a moment she was worried that they were going to sit on her, but they remained standing.

'. . . but that's not fair,' Dante was saying. He seemed upset.

'You gotta toughen up if you want to make it in this

industry,' replied his father.

'But I worked so hard on this role. I really feel like I got a hook on this character.'

'I know,' said Chase, who didn't look like he was enjoying the conversation any more than Dante was. 'You've done some great work on it but Callum was always only a small part. The film's about Petal.'

'But you're talking about cutting half of my scenes,' said Dante.

'Keep your voice down,' hissed Chase. 'Listen,' he said quietly, 'I'm doing this for your own good.'

'How can it be for my own good to cut my part out of the film?'

'Son, I'm only going to say this once and I don't want you to repeat it but the fact is . . .' He lowered his voice even more. 'The fact is . . . this is a lousy film.'

Dante stared in disbelief at what he was being told.

'I hoped it would be OK,' Chase continued, 'a kind of fun film about celebrity culture. But it's not. It's dross. It's garbage. I've been watching the rushes and there's no saving it. Every time I try to make it better, that girl comes along with some stupid idea to make it worse.'

'But you're the director,' said Dante.

'And her mum's the exec producer. I have to go along with it.'

'Isn't there anything that can be done?' asked Dante.

'Yes, I can save you,' said his father. 'The fact is that this is going to be the worst film of my career. I'll probably never direct again. It's going to stink so bad that anyone associated with it is going to carry the stench, me included. I don't want your career being damaged. That's why I'm cutting your role. OK?'

Dante took all this in then said, 'Thanks, Dad. I love you.' He hugged his father.

'I love you too, son,' said Chase.

'How sweet,' said Petal Moses, whose driver brought her buggy alongside them.

'Hold on, Mum,' she said into the mobile phone she was holding to her ear. 'Chase is here now. Hi, Chase. Mum says that it doesn't matter if I mime in time with the music because you'll be able to sort it out in the edit.'

'That's actually not so easy, Petal,' said Chase patiently.

'He says it's not that easy,' she said into the phone.

'Yes, I'll tell him.' She looked at him again. 'Mum says it *is* that easy and don't be so lazy, Chase, darling.'

Chase smiled. 'Sure thing, Petal. It's not a problem,' he said.

Chapter Fourteen

Dirk Dilly wasn't easily impressed. But standing on the Y of the Hollywood sign set in the hills above Los Angeles, he couldn't help but admire the view. It was early evening. The city lights stretched on for miles, reminding Dirk of the opening sequence to *The Big Zero*.

'Get yourself off that thing,' said Kitelsky, poking his head around the side of the W.

'Yeah, you get seen, we're all in trouble,' said Putz, looking through a huge O.

Dirk had noticed that, as the two Desert Dragons got nearer the city, they had become increasingly nervous about being seen.

'Right, let's get going,' said Dirk, jumping down.

'What? Now?' said Kitelsky.

'Maybe we should get a good night's sleep first,' said Putz.

'Whoever's stolen that film won't be sleeping,' said Dirk. 'Besides, it'll be easier to travel across the roofs at night.'

'Across the roofs?' said Putz.

'Of course,' said Dirk casually. 'Don't worry, city-dwelling humans don't look up much and most of these seem to be in cars.'

'But what if one of them does look up?' said Putz.

'If you get spotted, just stop and blend,' said Dirk. 'Humans are easily distracted. A song will come on the radio that they like, or they'll see something in a shop window, or they'll catch a whiff from a fast food joint and the memory of the shadow that passed overhead will vanish like that.' Dirk clicked his claws together and jumped on to an L.

'Blend? What you talking about?' said Putz. 'Desert Dragons can't blend.'

'Really? I didn't know that,' said Dirk innocently.

'You know full well that only Mountain Dragons can blend,' said Kitelsky.

'Then you'll just have to take your chances.

Unless . . .' Dirk paused.

'Unless what?' said Kitelsky.

'No, forget it,' replied Dirk.

'Unless what, Dilly?' repeated Kitelsky.

'Look, you two are quick but you don't know this environment. Me, I'm an urban-based Mountain Dragon. Why don't you stay here and keep look-out? I'll go find the tape and bring it back.'

'No way,' said Kitelsk. 'We're comin' wi' you.'

'Fair enough,' said Dirk, heading down the hill. 'Just remember to keep away from convertibles . . . oh, and watch out for window cleaners . . . and all those tall buildings in the financial area could cause a problem . . . and don't forget roof gardens . . .'

'Gee, Kitelsky,' said Putz. 'You know what he's talking about?'

'. . . and builders . . .' continued Dirk.

'It seems to me like this Mountain Dragon spends a lot of time around humans,' replied Kitelsky.

'. . . and astronomers can be a problem. They're always looking up,' added Dirk.

'Maybe we should leave it to him,' said Putz.

'I'm inclined to agree wi' you,' said Kitelsky.

'You're not coming?' said Dirk.

'Don't look so pleased,' said Kitelsky. 'We'll be here,

cooking up some fresh poison that's comin' your way if I smell so much as a whiff of double-crossin'.'

'You have my word as a dragon and as a detective,' said Dirk.

'We'll wait here by the sign,' said Putz.

'You'd better come and tell us when you find somethin',' said Kitelsky.

Dirk headed down the hill, where the trees got thicker and provided enough cover to move swiftly to the city.

One of the tricks of the trade that Dirk had picked up in his years working as a private detective was the ability to make a phone call without a phone. It was more difficult in London, where the telephone cables ran underground, but in Los Angeles they were raised on poles, giving Dirk easy access.

He landed on a roof next to a mast, in a quiet part of town. He reached out his right claw and connected to the wire. He held his left claw to his ear like he was holding a phone and adjusted his right until he heard a dialling tone. He tapped out the number Holly had given him and waited for an answer.

'Hello?' said a familiar voice.

'Hey, kiddo, it's me.'

'Dirk!' she exclaimed. 'Where are you?'

'Let's just say this isn't a long-distance call,' said Dirk.

'You're in LA?' said Holly.

'LA? Listen to you, you've gone all showbiz on me. How was your big film role?'

'It was strange.' She told him about the scene in Little Hope Village Hall then she said, 'How about you? Any clues about the film yet?'

'I've found the stars, a couple of Desert Dragons from out of town. A right pair of characters, not too friendly but they didn't seem to know anything about the filming.'

'So what's next?' asked Holly.

'Any ideas who the last person to see the film was?' asked Dirk.

'That would have been Theo,' replied Holly.

'Any other details?'

'Archie, Dirk's on the phone. Give me that card Theo gave you,' said Holly. 'Thanks. Theo Leggett, Assistant Director.' She read out the phone number.

'Holly and Archie, come down here immediately,' shouted Holly's dad in the background. 'We have dinner reservations and we've got to stop off at Mr Buchanan's first.'

'Coming,' shouted Holly. 'You don't think Buchanan's involved in this, do you?' she said into the receiver.

'We've got no reason to suspect him,' said Dirk.

'I suppose not,' said Holly. 'Archie says hi.'

'Hi to Archie,' replied Dirk. 'If the trail leads to Buchanan, I'll let you know, but I'm going to start with this Theo character. Nine times out of ten in my experience the last person to see something is the first person you suspect of having taken it. I'll speak soon.'

Dirk hung up and dialled Theo's number. It rang once then a nervous voice answered, 'Theo Leggett speaking. Hello?'

'Mr Leggett, my name's Dirk Dilly. I work for an insurance company,' said Dirk, doing his best to sound professional. 'I need to ask you a few questions.'

'What insurance company?' said Theo, a note of suspicion in his voice.

'Holly insurance,' replied Dirk, improvising as he went along. 'Holly of Hollywood. We cover the World Film Studios. I understand a tape went missing this morning.'

'I've never heard of you. Who is this?' demanded Theo.

'I told you, I'm –'

'Don't give me no story about an insurance company. I already spoke to the studio insurance people. He's put you up to this, hasn't he? Well, I told him that

I don't know who took the film and that's what I'm telling you. And I've never heard of no Mr Sorrentino. Now leave me alone.'

The phone went dead.

The sun was setting and the sky was turning mauve. Dirk felt a wave of exhaustion sweep over him. All in all it had been a long day. He decided to return to the hill for the night then make an early start in the morning.

He was bounding up the hill through the trees and had reached the Hollywood sign when a thorny weight landed on his back.

'Where you goin', Dilly?' said Kitelsky, his spikes digging into Dirk's back.

'Get off me,' growled Dirk. 'How many times do I have to say it? I'm trying to help. Where's Putz?'

Kitelsky released Dirk. 'He's down the hill, actin' a fool. Come on, I'll show you,' he said, walking into the trees.

Dirk opened his mouth and shot fire at Kitelsky's backside.

'Ow! What d'you go doin' that for?' said Kitelsky.

'That's a reminder not to go jumping on me again,' said Dirk.

They found Putz standing in a clearing, carefully

patting down a mound of old newspapers. He stood back, took aim, closed his eyes and blew. Bits of newspaper went flying everywhere.

'What's he doing?' asked Dirk.

'Tryin' to breathe fire,' replied Kitelsky, smirking.

Torn pages of newspaper fluttered back down to the ground.

'If you can do it, I can do it,' said Putz, seeing Dirk. 'We're dragons, ain't we? We got wings and teeth and claws and green blood. Ain't no reason why we can't breathe fire. Show me how you do it. I reckon I could learn easy.'

Dirk grabbed a sheet of newspaper from the ground, rolled it up and exhaled a thin line of fire, instantly igniting it.

'Looks easy enough,' said Putz, grabbing another couple of sheets and blowing on them. Instead of setting the paper on fire, he only managed to make it flap pathetically.

'I keep tellin' him that we ain't designed for fire-breathin',' said Kitelsky.

'Give me that,' said Dirk, snatching the paper from Putz's paws.

'Hey, mind your claws,' said Putz. 'I reckon I got close that time. I could feel my throat gettin' kinda warm.'

Dirk wasn't listening. He had opened the paper. It was a page of classified ads. At the bottom of the page was an advert that read:

Sorrentino Solutions

If you've got a problem, we'll find the solution

Chapter Fifteen

'It should be a right turn ... sorry, a left. No, a right,' said Big Hair.

'There it is,' said Holly, noticing a sign saying, 'Sands Mansion', with the Global Sands logo of a G and an S in a circle.

Mr Bigsby turned the car up the winding path through a gate that buzzed open automatically. In the car park were Mr Buchanan's silver Bentley and a yellow VW van.

'I won't be long,' said Holly's dad, parking the car and opening the door.

'Can't we come and have a look?' said Holly, eager to see what a billionaire's mansion looked like.

'We're already late for our dinner reservations,' said Big Hair.

'But we want to say thank you to Mr Buchanan for such an amazing holiday,' said Archie, winking at Holly.

Big Hair smiled. 'That's very sweet of you, Archie,' she said.

'OK, but you both need to be on your best behaviour,' said Mr Bigsby.

'Particularly you, Holly,' said Big Hair, who hadn't forgotten how Holly had broken into a high-security Global Sands animal-testing laboratory.

Holly wanted to protest but she felt Archie's hand on her arm. She kept quiet and stepped out of the car.

Sands Mansion overlooked the high-rise financial district of the city. It was an old-fashioned building with white walls and a grey stone roof. In front of it were layers of garden, each level symmetrically designed and immaculately maintained. Hundreds of security cameras covered the building, watching every square inch of the grounds.

'Nice pad,' said Archie. 'It reminds me of my second home. Or is it my third?'

'You're always getting those two mixed up,' said Holly.

Mr Buchanan appeared at the top of the steps with two scruffy-looking men wearing colourful T-shirts and flared trousers, one with a dark goatee beard, the other with a lighter under-chin beard. Brant Buchanan shook both their hands and said, 'Gentlemen, I'll see you tonight?' He handed the man with the under-chin beard a sealed envelope.

The two men shook his hand and said goodbye. As they passed Holly, the man with the goatee turned to Big Hair and said, 'How you doing?'

'Very well, thank you,' replied Big Hair primly, as though she had just been greeted by something that had come out of a dog's bottom.

'Malcolm,' said Mr Buchanan warmly. 'And Bridget.' He kissed the air next to Big Hair's cheeks. 'And the enigmatic Holly Bigsby.' He extended his hand.

Holly hesitated, still mistrustful of the billionaire.

'Holly,' said her father, with a warning tone.

Mr Buchanan smiled and turned to Archie. 'And I see you have a friend, Holly,' he said. 'It's so important for children to have company.'

'Are those hippies?' said Archie, pointing at the two men getting into the yellow van.'

Mr Buchanan laughed. 'In a way. They're conservationists. You see, I'm very interested in endangered animals. I contribute to a number of charities for lesser-spotted species.'

'Oh, Brant,' sighed Big Hair, 'the world is a better place for philanthropists such as yourself.'

'What's a philanthropist?' asked Archie.

'Someone who uses their money to do good,' said Mr Bigsby.

Brant Buchanan led them down the steps towards the mansion, past an ornate fountain.

'It's a wonderful building,' said Big Hair. 'Who designed it?'

'A very famous architect whose name completely eludes me,' said Mr Buchanan. 'I do recall that it was built in 1924.'

They turned a corner, finding themselves in front of a large cylindrical building surrounded by scaffolding.

'Of course the disadvantage of an old building is that we often need repairs such as this,' said Buchanan. He looked at Holly and said, 'Actually, this is an interesting part of the building. Come and have a look.'

Mr Buchanan pulled a sheet of tarpaulin to one side and motioned them into the room.

'Cool room,' said Archie as they stepped inside.

The curved walls were filled with rows and rows of

books from the wooden floors right up to the glass ceiling.

'What a beautiful space,' said Big Hair.

'It was built as a place to store coal apparently, which is why it has no windows. So I put in the glass roof and converted it into a library,' said Mr Buchanan.

'It's an impressive collection,' said Holly's dad.

'Thank you,' replied Mr Buchanan. 'There are some very valuable books here. I'm afraid you won't find any novels or poetry though. I have to admit I don't have much time for fiction. I always say, there's so much remarkable fact, why make things up? In fact, look.' He grabbed a book from the shelf and handed it to Big Hair. 'You were asking about the building. This gives you its history. Please borrow it.'

'Thank you very much,' said Big Hair.

'I tell you what,' continued Mr Buchanan, 'why don't you dine here tomorrow night? I can show you around properly, you can tell me what you've learnt about my home, and Malcolm and I can discuss boring business matters then instead.'

'Will the work wait until tomorrow?' asked Holly's dad.

'Of course,' replied Mr Buchanan, leading them out of the library and back towards the car. 'I'll see all of you at seven o'clock tomorrow.'

Back in the car, on the way to the restaurant, Big Hair said, 'How kind of Brant. He is a remarkable man.'

'I don't understand it,' said Mr Bigsby. 'He flew me five thousand miles urgently and I haven't had one thing to do since being here.'

'Don't complain, Malcolm,' scolded Big Hair. 'When you work for a man like Brant, this is the kind of treatment you can expect.'

Chapter Sixteen

irk, Kitelsky and Putz spent the night on the hill overlooking Los Angeles, taking turns to stay awake and keep watch for humans. Dirk took the first shift then settled down by Kitelsky, leaving Putz on look-out duty.

It had been a long day and Dirk fell asleep instantly. He dreamt that he was in a film version of *St George and the Dragon*, in which he was playing the knight opposite Brant Buchanan as the dragon. In the dream an unseen director kept shouting at Dirk for forgetting his one line, which was 'Die, dragon, die!'

When he woke up, the sky had turned a hazy yellow and the vast city was half hidden by heavy smog.

Both Kitelsky and Putz were sleeping, curled up with their spikes on the outside, looking like two dense patches of cactuses.

Dirk stretched, and his back made an alarming clicking noise. He yawned and picked up the piece of newspaper with the phone number for Sorrentino Solutions, then tiptoed away.

He made his way down the hill and then across the roofs to the same spot by the telephone mast. He connected using his claws and carefully tapped out the number.

An answerphone message kicked in: 'This is Sorrentino Solutions. If you want to speak to us, that's just fine, but call us back after nine,' said a chipper female voice.

Dirk hung up and waited, gazing at the rooftops, mulling over the case. The film had been out there for twenty-four hours. For all he knew it was already too late. If it got into the media's hands, it would be picked up by every news channel and chat show in the world. It would be big news.

Dirk could see a wall-clock inside one of the houses but he had never been much good at telling the time, so he was pleased when a woman in a tracksuit came out of the house, walked to her enormous four-wheel drive SUV and shouted, 'Come on, kids. It's nine o'clock already.'

Dirk connected to the phone line and called the number again.

'If you've got a problem, be it awful or gruesome, pick up the phone and call Sorrentino Solutions. Sandra speaking. How can I help you?' said the receptionist.

'I'm sorry?' said Dirk.

'You don't like it? What about this?' chirruped Sandra. 'If you've got problems, big or small, let Sorrentino Solutions solve them all.'

'Excellent,' said Dirk. 'I wonder if you can help me.'

'I'll certainly do my best, sir.'

'I'm supposed to be delivering a parcel to you this morning,' said Dirk, 'and I've got this number but I think they've given me the wrong address.'

Sandra gave him the address and directions and he made his way there.

He came to a stop on top of a cinema that showed old black and white films, from which he could see into the ground-floor office of Sorrentino Solutions, where the blonde receptionist was sat behind a large bunch of daffodils. On the wall was a painting of more daffodils and when she got up to make herself a coffee, Dirk noticed that she even had a daffodil pattern on her skirt.

She picked up the phone. Dirk grabbed a telephone wire that ran across the road, over the roof he was resting on, and connected his claw. He located the line into the building, and listened in on the phone conversation.

'I'm sorry, sir, Mr Sorrentino isn't available right now,' Sandra was saying. 'Can I take a message?'

'Yes,' said the man on the line. 'Tell him I'm not going to pay any more than the agreed price.'

'I'll pass on the message,' said Sandra, who must have been lying about her boss being busy because when the next call came through from a Mr Smith she said, 'Just one moment, please . . .' There was a click then, 'Mr Sorrentino, there's another Mr Smith on the line. Oh, and Mr Tanner phoned and said he won't increase his offer.'

'Thank you, Sandra,' said Sorrentino. He spoke quickly in a clipped American accent. 'So, Mr Smith, what's your problem?'

'It's my neighbour's dog. He keeps urinating against my fence,' said Mr Smith.

'I see, and you want me to teach the little pooch a lesson?' replied Sorrentino.

'Yeah, I do. Dumb dog!' said Mr Smith.

Throughout the day Sorrentino had a number of calls along similar lines. The clients would tell him their problems, which ranged from petty parking disputes right up to one caller who wanted to put a family-run cookie shop out of business so he could buy their premises and turn them into a new hotel complex.

In each case Mr Sorrentino would listen, take down all the details, then give the client his rates and assure them of his utmost discretion, without showing any sign of caring about the consequences of his actions.

In between work calls, Sandra had long gossipy phone conversations with her sister about her boyfriend, Clive, who was an out-of-work actor and hadn't landed a part for several months.

'I wouldn't mind but there's only so far my wages will stretch,' said Sandra.

'Ask Mr Sorrentino for a pay rise,' replied her sister. 'You keep saying how well business is going. I still don't understand what he does.'

'To tell the truth, nor do I,' said Sandra, giggling. 'But I'm sure it's really boring, probably to do with computers or something. He does have a lot of Mr Smiths phoning up though.'

At one o'clock Sandra walked to the bank to pay in cheques, then bought herself some lunch and returned to the office for the rest of the afternoon. At five-thirty she left. Dirk stayed where he was.

After she had gone Mr Sorrentino made one more call.

'Hey, man,' said a voice.

'It's me,' said Sorrentino. 'You got the money?'

'Yeah, man, we got the cash.'

'Good. Meet me on the top level of the parking lot by the Grove shopping complex in half an hour,' said Sorrentino.

Dirk looked across the road at the multi-storey car park with GROVE printed down the side. He waited for Sorrentino to appear. The day's eavesdropping had left Dirk with a mental image of what he would look like. From his voice he pictured a man in his forties, maybe pushing fifty, with stubble and dark, uncaring eyes. But no such man appeared. In fact no one came out of the building.

Dirk knew that if he was in Sorrentino's line of business he certainly wouldn't want to make it easy for people to find him. Figuring there was a back door to the building, he decided to catch up with him at the meeting point.

Dirk checked there was no one looking up then sprang from the roof, flying across the road, along the top of a market place and up to a department store. In the middle of the shopping centre was a fountain sending out spurts of water in time with music which was being piped out of speakers. Shopping-laden humans were milling around. None of them noticed Dirk flying over their heads, somersaulting in mid-air and landing softly in a crouching position behind a large rubbish bin in the other corner of the highest level of the car park.

It was empty. Dirk heard a car engine approaching. A yellow VW van drove up the ramp and did a circuit of the level before stopping in front of the lift doors.

The car stopped and two men with long hair and flared trousers stepped out.

'You there, Sorrentino?' said one of the men.

A bright flashlight was switched on from the shadow beside the lift. The two men shielded their eyes. 'What's with the interrogation lights, man?' said the other.

'That's far enough,' said Sorrentino, from behind the light. 'Let's see the money.'

The man with the under-chin beard pulled out an envelope and made to walk forward.

'Throw it,' said Sorrentino.

The man threw the envelope into the shadow. After a moment's pause a suitcase slid out into the light.

'This better be worth the money,' said the man.

'If you're not satisfied, you've got my number,' said Sorrentino.

'Well, it was a pleasure doing business with you, man,' said the man with the goatee beard and both of them got back into the van and left.

With no reason to follow the van, Dirk waited for Mr Sorrentino to show himself, wondering again whether he was going to match the image he had built up in his head. The flashlight went off. Dirk saw a movement in the shadow by the lift. Then Sorrentino stepped into the light, revealing his face. He had a long nose, yellow eyes, and his grey skin was covered in thin white spikes.

'So Sorrentino's a Desert Dragon,' muttered Dirk to himself.

Chapter Seventeen

irk watched the Desert Dragon emerge from the
shadows and peer over the edge of the car park.

'Pretty view,' said Dirk, stepping out from behind
the bin.

Sorrentino spun around. 'Who are you?' he
demanded.

'The name's Dirk Dilly,' Dirk replied. 'And I didn't
catch your first name.'

'My name's Mo. Mo Sorrentino. What's it to you,
Mountain Dragon?'

'Mo? You're the dragon Kitelsky and Putz mentioned,' said Dirk, approaching on all fours, with his
head lowered.

'How do know Kitelsky and Putz?' snarled Sorrentino, sidestepping in the same way Dirk had seen the other Desert Dragons do.

'Don't you ever worry about all those human lives you ruin?' said Dirk.

'Listen, I make some people happy, I make some people sad. What business is it of yours, anyway?' Sorrentino said, flicking out his claws threateningly.

'None at all,' said Dirk, 'but films of dragons make it my business.'

'Ah, so that's what this is about,' said Sorrentino.

'What's your involvement, Sorrentino?' said Dirk, thick clouds of smoke gushing from his nose.

'Your fire don't scare me, Mountain Dragon,' said Sorrentino, moving so he was within spitting distance of Dirk's face.

Dirk could hear a bubbling noise coming from his throat.

'I know what you're thinking,' said Sorrentino. 'Is he loaded with his day's poison? And to tell you the truth, I've kind of forgotten myself, but being as Desert Dragon poison is the most deadly in the world, you've got to ask yourself a question. Do I feel lucky? Well, do you? Do you, Dirk?'

'You watch too many movies, Mo,' replied Dirk. 'If

you killed me here, you'd have to dispose of the body and I'm guessing you could do without that kind of hassle. Where's the film?'

'Ah, who cares? I got paid already,' replied the Desert Dragon. 'I sold it, so what?'

'Sold it? What do you think you're playing at, Sorrentino? Do you want to start a war?'

'A war?' sneered Sorrentino. 'Come on, if you knew humans like I do you'd know they've caught weirder things on tape.' He laughed. 'This isn't the Middle Ages. People don't believe in us any more. One little film ain't gonna change that.'

'Who did you sell it to?' said Dirk.

'You just watched them drive away. They paid well too, more than I was expectin' to get. Go ahead and get it back if you want, but I'd hurry, if I were you.'

Dirk snarled. He ran to the edge of the car park and looked down. The yellow van had left the car park and was waiting at the lights.

'This isn't the last you've seen of me,' he said to Sorrentino.

'Do me a favour, call my receptionist and make an appointment next time,' replied the Desert Dragon.

Dirk sent an angry burst of fire at Sorrentino and flew down to a nearby building.

Jumping over roofs, he followed the van across town. It was making slow progress with the rush-hour traffic, but after a while, the van turned off the main road, took a right, then a left, turning up a winding private road, which had a sign that said 'Sands Mansion' – with a logo that Dirk recognised at once as belonging to Brant Buchanan's company, Global Sands.

'Super-rich rats,' Dirk swore.

A row of security cameras lined the top of the gate. Dirk could go no further.

Had Dirk been able to follow the van into the grounds of Sands Mansion he would have seen Brant Buchanan lead Hunter and Frank into a cylindrical building surrounded by scaffolding.

'Nice library, man,' said Frank. 'You having work done?

'I'm having some extra security measures put in,' replied Buchanan, striding across the room and reaching for a book on a high shelf with a red spine and a tiny speck of white at the bottom.

'Hey, I recognise that spine,' said Hunter, pulling out his own copy from his jacket pocket. 'It's *Dragonlore* by Ivor Klingerflim.'

'Indeed,' said Brant Buchanan, tilting the book. 'Except that this is just the cover.'

Four shelves of books on the other side of the wall flickered and disappeared. What had looked like a row of book spines revealed itself to be a projection on a TV screen. The screen went blank.

'Man, that's neat,' said Frank.

Weaver stepped into the room and handed Mr Buchanan a disk from his pocket. 'I've transferred the tape,' he said.

Buchanan reached down and found a book spine by an author called David Player. He pressed a hidden button on it and a drawer slid open. He inserted the disk, the drawer closed and all the letters lit up on the author's name except for the a and i in David.

'Hey, DVD player. That's clever, man,' said Hunter.

'One of Weaver's little jokes,' said Buchanan. 'Now let's see what we've got, shall we?'

A desert appeared on the screen. The sound of whistling wind filled the room. The shot panned across a desolate landscape dotted with strange trees with thick twisted branches. '*That's nice. Hold that,*' said a voice on the tape and the camera stopped moving. '*Go in a little,*' said the voice. The camera zoomed in. Something moved in the shot. It was as though two of the strange trees were shifting in the distance. '*What's that?*' said the voice. The camera zoomed in again. The picture fell out of focus for a moment and then refocused on the hazy horizon, where two cactus-like creatures were fighting.

'What do you think?' asked Hunter excitedly.

'Yeah, what do you think, man?' said Frank enthusiastically.

As usual, Brant Buchanan chose his words carefully. 'It's a bit blurry, isn't it?' he said.

'Blurry?' exclaimed Frank, leaping in front of the screen. 'We bring you never-seen-before footage of two Desert Dragons filmed yesterday and you call it blurry?'

'Calm down, man,' said Hunter, anxious not to upset the billionaire.

'I am calm. I just think he should appreciate what we've got here. This is solid-gold proof, man.'

Buchanan laughed. 'Gentlemen,' he said, 'I thought I made it perfectly clear when I employed you that I have no doubt of the existence of dragons. None whatsoever. Please don't get me wrong. This footage will serve its purpose but, you see, I do not need further proof.'

He swapped the DVD with another from his pocket

and the desert footage disappeared and was replaced by a map of the world.

'From Ivor Klingerflim's book we know that there are dragons in every corner of the earth. Varieties of the Desert Dragons you showed me exist not only in California, but in the Sahara, the Arabian, the Gobi . . . In fact, they reside in every great desert of the world.'

As he spoke, the map lit up the world's deserts.

'There are Mountain Dragons wherever there are mountains.'

This time mountains of the world lit up.

'The oceans are full of Sea Dragons and other even more fantastic beasts. The forests and jungles are alive with as many varieties of Tree Dragon as there are varieties of trees. The Arctic and Antarctic are rich with Snow Dragons. The sky itself is littered with sub-limated Sky Dragons hiding amongst the clouds.'

By the time he had finished speaking the entire map was lit up. It was so bright that Hunter and Frank had to shield their eyes.

The screen went blank.

'There are even a few urban-based dragons,' said Buchanan.

The screen showed a dragon creeping around an office.

'Woo, man,' said Frank.

'You got an extreme close-up,' said Hunter, running his fingers through his greasy hair.

'But if you got stuff this good, why do you need us?' said Frank.

'I have employed you because I need more information. *Dragonlore* is not enough. I want to know everything there is to know about dragons,' said Buchanan.

'OK, but can I ask why, man?' said Hunter.

'Because, shortly, I intend to catch one,' replied the billionaire.

Chapter Eighteen

As a thank you for the long day of filming, World Studios had given all the extras from the school concert scene free VIP passes to the movie theme park next door.

Mr Bigsby and his wife had dropped Holly and Archie at the gates and gone shopping, saying they would pick them up in time for dinner at Brant Buchanan's mansion in the evening.

The theme park was brilliant. All of the rides were based on films. There was loads to do and it was all free. Even better, the VIP tickets meant that wherever there was a long queue, Holly and Archie could jump it and whenever they fancied a snack they didn't have to pay.

'This is the best holiday ever,' Holly said as they entered an open-air walk-through jungle full of moving models of dinosaurs called Dinoworld.

'I'm here in the jungle with the lesser-spotted Holly Bigsby,' said Archie, using the ice cream he was eating as a microphone. 'Holly, tell me what it's like being a VIP.'

'I think it's very V to be a VIP,' said Holly.

'So you're saying that it's V V to be a VIP?'

'If not V V V,' replied Holly, laughing.

'This model represents a dimetrodon,' said a young American boy with an extremely large head and an annoyingly loud voice, pointing at a plastic lizard beneath a plant. The lizard scuttled unconvincingly across the rock. 'Interestingly, although it looks like a dinosaur it is actually an ancestor of the mammals,' continued the boy with a self-satisfied smile.

Holly and Archie moved quickly to the next section, but the boy followed them. 'We're now entering the Triassic period, in which dinosaurs first appeared,' he said.

A long-necked dinosaur loomed over them, its neck moving mechanically and a strange roaring coming from a speaker by its side.

'This is a plateosaurus,' said the boy, who was beginning to get on Holly's nerves. 'And over here is the pterosaur, a flying reptile. And here is a . . . oh, that's not right. This isn't a dinosaur.'

Holly and Archie looked at the model the boy was pointing at.

'Dinosaurs don't have smoke coming out of their noses and they certainly weren't red and green.'

Holly gasped and Archie almost dropped his ice cream. Standing frozen to the spot, moving his head robotically, was Dirk.

'How do you know what colour they were?' said Archie. 'They could have been bright pink for all anyone knows. All they've ever found is bones.'

'Well, that's not a dinosaur. It's a dragon and that's stupid because dragons don't exist,' said the boy, stamping his feet.

Dirk paused then moved to look at the boy. 'No one likes a know-it-all. Beat it, kid,' he said.

'Th . . . th . . . that's so rude,' stammered the boy, bursting into tears and running away.

'Dirk!' said Holly, throwing her arms around his neck.

'And you're right, Archie, some of them were pink,' said Dirk.

'You remember dinosaurs?' said Archie.

'I'm not that old,' replied Dirk, 'but I once met a dragon that claimed to have kept a pink tyrannosaurus rex as a pet. It was very loyal apparently but it did bite.'

'What are you doing here?' asked Holly.

'Buchanan's got the film,' said Dirk.

'Buchanan?' said Holly.

A group of Japanese tourists entered. Dirk froze and went back to his small robotic head movements.

'Ooooh!' they said, seeing him. 'Will you take a photo of us?' said one of the tourists, handing a camera to Holly.

'Sure,' she said.

They gathered around Dirk, and Holly took the photo, but instead of taking a picture, she pressed the off button.

'That's a good one,' she said, handing the camera back to the grateful tourists, who thanked her and moved on.

'So Buchanan is involved,' said Holly.

'Seems so. Sorrentino sold him the film,' said Dirk.

'Who's Sorrentino?' asked Holly.

'He's a dragon who hires himself out to humans to solve their problems.'

'It sounds like what you do,' said Holly.

'Yeah, except he doesn't mind people getting hurt . . . oh, and he's got a receptionist.'

'You've got Mrs Klingerflim,' said Holly.

Dirk laughed then froze again as a mother and her two children walked past. Once they had gone, Holly continued, 'You think Buchanan knows about you and me? I mean, Dad hasn't exactly been busy since he's been here. If Buchanan suspects I know a dragon, he could be using me to get to you.'

'We'll need to be extremely careful,' said Dirk, 'but I do need to get that film back.'

'The mansion's covered in cameras,' said Holly.

'Even the security cameras are watched by security cameras,' added Archie.

'We're going round for dinner,' said Holly. 'We could find out where he's keeping it.'

'Good,' said Dirk, 'but be cautious. No blending. We can't take any risks if there's the slightest possibility that Buchanan suspects that you have a connection to me.'

'OK,' said Holly.

'And if I'm going to find a way in, I could do with some details about the mansion,' said Dirk.

'Buchanan gave Big Hair that book about its history,' said Archie.

'Great. I'll come and see you later tonight at your house to pick up the book,' said Dirk. 'In the meantime I'm going to keep an eye on the two guys he's got working for him.'

'We'll find the tape,' said Holly.

'Good work, but don't let him find out what you're doing. Make it look like a game,' said Dirk. 'Now, I'd better get out of here. I'll see you tonight.'

Holly squeezed his right paw. 'Bye, Dirk,' she said.

'Hey, little lady, no touching the exhibits,' said an official in a T-shirt with 'Dinoworld' written on the front. 'Some of them might bite,' he added, with a false laugh. 'No, but seriously, you really shouldn't touch them . . . Hey, I don't remember this fella.' He looked at Dirk. 'This fella's more like a dragon than a dinosaur, isn't he?' He reached up and pinched the skin on Dirk's cheek. 'How do they make them so realistic?'

A low growl came from Dirk's throat.

'I thought you said no touching,' said Holly.

'You're quite right, little lady,' said the man, moving his hand away.

'Can you show us the way out?' asked Archie. 'We're lost.'

'Sure, follow me. It's right out of Triassic, past

143

Jurassic and you're into the canteen where you can feast on one of our terrific dinoburgers. Don't worry, they're not made from real dinosaur,' he said, sounding like he was reading from a script.

Dirk waited until they were out of sight before jumping up to the roof of the Haunted House.

'Look, Mum, a dragon,' said a little girl holding a lollipop.

'Yes, lovely, dear, you've seen all sorts of things today, haven't you?' replied her mother.

Chapter Nineteen

At dinner at Brant Buchanan's that evening Holly tried hard to be on her best behaviour. She managed to be polite as they arrived at the mansion and as they took their places around the impressive table in the centre of the cavernous dining hall. A waiter brought in the starters and announced that everyone would be eating foie gras except for Holly, who was a vegetarian and was served asparagus.

Archie found it funny the way the waiter said foie gras in a French accent and asked, 'What's fwa grar then?'

'It's a kind of pâté,' explained Mr Buchanan. 'It's made from a duck's liver that has been enlarged by force-feeding the animal before slaughter.' The billionaire scooped up a bit on a wafer and ate it. 'Delicious,' he said.

'That's so cruel,' exclaimed Holly, unable to contain herself. 'Only a monster would do something like that.'

'Holly,' said her father, glaring at her.

'It's fine, Malcolm,' said Mr Buchanan. 'We are all entitled to our opinions. Some do find the process rather barbaric, but then, I say, why is it any worse than wringing a chicken's neck? In which case, are you saying that all meat eaters are monsters?'

Holly looked at Archie, who had a piece of the pâté held up to his mouth. She scowled at him.

He put it back down guiltily.

Holly turned back to Mr Buchanan. 'It's worse because you're not just killing the animal, you're torturing the poor thing first. It's as bad as the experiments you do on animals.'

'So, I hear Global Sands stock went up this morning,' said Mr Bigsby, trying desperately to change the subject.

'Yes, it's been a good day for us,' replied Mr Buchanan.

For the rest of the meal, the adults went on about

146

inflation and real estate and emerging markets and all the other boring things that adults talk about. Holly and Archie talked amongst themselves. After dessert, Mr Buchanan suggested that they retire to the lounge for coffee.

'Can we go and look around?' asked Holly.

'Feel free,' said Buchanan. 'I'm afraid that having no children myself I have no toys or computer games but I'm sure you can find some way to amuse yourselves.'

As they left the room and headed up the stairs, Archie said, 'That was easy.'

It was a huge mansion. They took one room each, trying to make it look like they were playing a game of hide-and-seek, searching for places to hide. The rooms were stylishly but sparsely decorated, which made them quick to check, and it wasn't long before they were heading back downstairs. But the search downstairs proved equally fruitless.

'The problem is we're looking for a reel of film but it could be anything by now – a DVD, an MP3, anything,' said Archie.

'I know but we've still got to try,' said Holly.

'Where's left?' asked Archie.

'The library,' said Holly.

They found their way out of the main building,

across the floodlit courtyard to the cylindrical building surrounded by scaffolding.

They pushed the tarpaulin back and found that the door was unlocked. Holly stepped inside and looked up at the night sky, through the glass ceiling. Archie flicked the light switch on, illuminating the curved walls of books.

'Have you noticed something odd?' said Holly, looking up.

'What?'

'There are no cameras.'

Archie saw she was right. Unlike every other room in the building there wasn't a single security camera.

'But didn't he say that it was full of expensive books? Why wouldn't he have cameras?'

'Because he's got something to hide,' replied Holly. 'Look for a clue.'

There were books on everything from fly-fishing to fencing, histories of every country in the world, biographies of great leaders, explanations of astrology, astronomy, mythology. In fact, every subject in the world. Then something caught Holly's eye. It was a red book spine with a small triangle of white at the bottom. It was sticking out slightly on a high shelf just out of reach.

'*Dragonlore*,' she gasped, trying to jump and reach the book. 'It's too high up.'

'Try this,' said Archie, pulling out four larger books from a lower shelf and placing them on top of each other.

Holly stood on top of the pile and grabbed the spine of the book. She tried to pull it out. 'It's stuck,' she said, only succeeding in tilting it at an angle.

'It's not a book, it's a switch,' said Archie.

A section of books had vanished, revealing a blank screen. The screen flickered and then a desert landscape appeared.

'It's the film,' said Holly.

They watched as the camera moved across the scene. They heard Theo Leggett's voice giving instructions to the cameraman. The shot zoomed in and found the two spiky dragons moving on the shimmering horizon, sending clouds of dust up as they fought.

'That's so cool,' said Archie.

'But where's the actual film?' said Holly.

A voice outside interrupted them. 'Holly, Archie, come along now. It's time to go home.' It was Big Hair.

'Come on, we'd better put everything back,' said Archie.

'But we haven't found the film,' protested Holly.

'At least we know it's in here somewhere,' said Archie.

Holly pushed the false book back and replaced the other books as they had found them.

The desert disappeared and, once again, was replaced by the image of book spines.

Holly and Archie went back into the main building, where the others were standing in the hall.

'I trust that you found a way to amuse yourselves in my stuffy old house,' said Mr Buchanan.

'We played hide-and-seek,' said Holly.

'It was fun,' added Archie.

'I'm glad it wasn't too boring for you,' replied the billionaire.

Chapter Twenty

Following the yellow van across town, Dirk found he was enjoying himself. As he leapt from roof to roof, he recited the opening lines from the voice-over that ran through *The Big Zero*.

'In some stories,' Dirk muttered, 'the kind they like to tell you in Hollywood, the good guys always win and the bad guys always lose. Well, I live in the real Hollywood and I can tell you that in real life it ain't like that. In my experience, the bad guys get their fair share of winning too.'

The van parked in a side street and the two long-haired men in flared trousers stepped out.

'All I'm saying is that we got to give Buchanan

something really good, Frank, man,' said Hunter.

'That's what I'm talking about,' replied Frank, slamming the car door shut. 'It was a classic cover-up story – no pictures, no one remembers what happened. He's the most reliable source we got.'

'Reliable? I think we must have different dictionaries, man.'

'You know what I mean, Hunter.'

The two men walked to the end of the road, where there was a bookshop called Unknown Worlds. Outside, a man in a mushroom hat strummed a guitar underneath some wind chimes. As Hunter and Frank entered the shop, Dirk caught a whiff of burning incense. Dirk knew the sort of place. Inside would be material on every conspiracy theory known to man. There would be books on angels, fairies, aliens and dragons and not one word of fact in any of them.

When they came out, Frank was carrying a large pile of books.

'I don't know why you waste your time on this, man,' said Hunter. 'When it comes to dragons, there's only one book you need.' He pulled out a battered copy of *Dragonlore* from his pocket and waved it in Frank's face.

'Yeah, but what about . . .' Frank lowered his voice,

'the Turning Stone, man. Imagine the sort of money Buchanan would pay for that! We could move out of our mums' houses, and set up the business properly, man. A proper office, rather than the back room of a laundrette.'

'We got to give him something solid,' said Hunter.

Frank stopped. 'Well, you know what I think? I think Minertia had it. I think she buried it with the rest of her treasure.'

'Hidden treasure. Man, I worry about you sometimes. How are we going to ever get taken seriously with you going on about hidden treasure and alien cats?'

'I believe what I believe, man. Find Minertia's treasure, you find the Turning Stone, man.'

Hunter picked up the top book from the pile that Frank was carrying. 'And you're going to find it in *Men are from Mars, Dragons are from Pluto*, man? You're hopping down mad alley in crazy town, Frank.'

The two men reached the car and Hunter opened the door so Frank could climb in with his books.

Dirk's mind was racing. He knew the Turning Stone was real. It was said that whoever possessed it would have power over all dragonkind. So was Frank's theory so crazy? It made sense that Minertia would have had it. That would explain why Vainclaw and Karnataka were desperate to get their hands on Minertia's treasure. Karnataka's words came back to him. '*If you knew what I know, knowing you, you'd be looking for it too . . .*' and, '*If you knew what I know, you wouldn't help me find it.*' Of course! Karnataka knew about the Turning Stone and he knew that Dirk wouldn't trust him with something so powerful any more than he would trust Vainclaw with it.

'Hey, Hunter, that cat's looking at me.'

A tabby cat was scratching itself against a nearby wall.

'Don't act wacko, man,' said Hunter.

'It's got alien eyes, man, alien eyes,' said Frank, slamming the door shut.

'You know, you got to get past the cat thing,' said Hunter, getting into the driver's seat. 'It's holding you back, man.'

When Holly and Archie arrived back at the house, they ran upstairs to Holly's room, shut the door and went out on to the balcony.

'Dirk?' said Holly.

'I'm blended on the roof above you,' said Dirk. 'We need to be quick. I don't want to take any unnecessary risks. What news?'

'It's in the round building surrounded by scaffolding,' said Holly. 'There are cameras all around but none inside. We guess Buchanan doesn't want anyone seeing what happens in there.'

'Any indication that he suspects you?' asked Dirk.

'No. He let us run around wherever we wanted,' said Holly. 'If he knew about you and me, he'd be more cautious, wouldn't he?'

'Unless he wanted you to find the film,' said Dirk.

'But it was you that discovered he had the film, not us,' said Archie.

'True, but still be careful, both of you,' said Dirk. 'We shouldn't meet again. It's too risky.'

'I've got the book for you,' said Archie, pulling out the history of Sands Mansion.

'Hold it up,' said Dirk.

Archie did so and Dirk's red tail dropped into view, wrapped itself around the book and took it. 'Thanks,' he said.

'Will you go and get it tonight?' said Holly.

'No. I'll need time to study the book and work out a way around the cameras,' said Dirk. 'My guess is that a man like Buchanan won't go public with this straight away. Besides, something else has come up. I'm going to be out of town for a couple of days.'

'Isn't that a bit of a gamble?' said Archie.

'Maybe, but my gut tells me that anyone as wealthy as Buchanan is going to want to keep a secret like this to himself for a while.'

'Where are you going?' asked Archie.

'I'm going underground,' said Dirk.

Chapter Twenty-One

Just outside the city, in a quiet spot, Dirk came to a standstill on a suitable rock and politely asked it to take him down. The rock, being rock, obliged unquestioningly.

He travelled for a while in darkness and then the orange glow of earthlight filled the sphere of shifting stone, making it possible to read the book Archie had given him. Past the lithosphere tunnel it grew lighter and the heat became uncomfortable. The pages of the book turned brown as the heat cooked them. As Dirk turned the last page, the whole book crumbled to ash. Still, he had read enough.

Eventually, Dirk felt the rock beneath him pull

away. He braced himself, remembering how hot the banks of the Outer Core had been the last time he visited. As he felt himself tumble down, he curled up into a ball, protecting his soft underbelly from the scorching pebbles by the fiery lake that hissed and bubbled angrily. He sprang to his feet and headed along the beach.

The Outer Core wasn't exactly a popular tourist retreat and for some time Dirk walked without seeing a soul. Eventually he found the wingless Firedrake sitting by the lakeside, using a long-handled ladle to fill a line of flasks with the contents of the lake. The Firedrake had tough skin, with rows of tiny holes on its back. A pair of crudely fashioned sunglasses, made from the same black metal as the ladle and flasks, rested on his upturned nose.

'Shute Hobcraft,' said Dirk.

'Dirk Dilly, dude,' replied the Firedrake, looking up. 'Watch this.'

Shute picked up one of the flasks, opened it and poured its scalding contents into his mouth. He crouched down, with a look of concentration on his face, and suddenly a jet of steam shot from a hole on the lower part of his back with such force that it propelled him forward. Dirk dodged out of the way as the

Firedrake whizzed past him, spinning over and landing upside down on the beach in fits of giggles.

'What a rush, dude. Help me up, will you, Dirk?'

Dirk pulled Shute to his feet.

'Still taking your job seriously, then,' said Dirk.

'Hey, I can't help it if I make work fun,' said Shute.

Shute Hobcraft's job was to check how hot the Outer Core was. The slightest drop in temperature meant that there was a dragon in it, and that a banished dragon was trying to escape from the Inner Core. If this happened, Shute would alert the authorities, who would catch the escapee.

'I've come to ask you about Minertia,' said Dirk.

'Oh yeah, dude, she was one big dragon.'

'You were the last one to see her before she was sent down. Any idea what she did with her treasure?' asked Dirk.

'You're not the first to ask me,' said Shute. 'Every so often, some gold-greedy dragon comes asking about it. The last time it was a Mountain Dragon, like yourself, and a Sea Dragon. I forget their names.'

'Jegsy and Flotsam?' asked Dirk.

'That was them,' said Shute. 'They seemed like bad sorts to me, dude, but I didn't think looting was your bag, Dirk.'

159

'It's not. I don't care about the gold,' said Dirk.

'Well, I can't help. I've no idea what she did with it.' Shute downed the contents of the flask. Steam shot from all of the holes on his back. 'Woo hoo, that's hot,' he said.

'Did she say anything to you at all?'

'She was more of a thinker than a speaker. She could read your mind, you know,' said Shute. 'I was wondering why she didn't try to make a run for it, because she only had three Drakes holding her down and, like I say, she was a fair-sized dragon. She turned to me and I heard her speak in my head: "I helped define these laws. I will not break them." Then she jumped straight in, not a second thought. It was pretty mad to watch.'

'That's all she said?' said Dirk.

'Sorry, dude.'

'Rats!' said Dirk, wondering what to do next.

'You could go and ask her, I guess,' said Shute.

'What do you mean?' asked Dirk.

'I mean, if I really wanted to know something like that I'd swim down to the Inner Core and ask her. She wouldn't tell you if you were a gold-digger but she might if you had good intentions . . . providing she's still alive.'

'You're crazy. Swim down through that?' said Dirk, stepping back from the lake. 'I'd die.'

'Die, dude?' said Shute. 'No way, this is the life force. Sure, it's hot. I'm not saying it won't sting a little but it won't kill you. It's where we all start life, isn't it?' Shute threw an empty flask into the lake. As it hit the surface, red boiling liquid splashed back and the flask sank, sending black smoke up.

Dirk walked to the edge of the lake and looked in. He tried to think of an option that didn't involve having to swim through it. He could simply walk away and hope that Vainclaw had no better luck finding the Turning Stone. But Vainclaw wouldn't give up so easily, and if he found it, then what? Ultimate war. And if Shute was right that Minertia could read minds, then she would know he didn't want it for himself. He looked at the scorching lake with grim determination.

'Hey, dude, you're going to do it, aren't you? That's what I like about you, dude. You're a thrill-seeker like me,' said Shute gleefully. 'Don't worry, I won't call the Dragnet on you. I'll allow for two heat dips, one when you go down, another when you come back up.'

Dirk dipped a claw into the lava. It wasn't too bad.

He tried a paw.

'Grearrghouch!' he screeched. 'Rats in grass skirts, that's hot!'

'The trick is to just jump straight in,' said Shute.

'See you round, Shute,' said Dirk, gritting his teeth and wading into the lake.

The scorching liquid surrounded him, scalding the skin on his legs. Dirk took a deep breath and dived in, fully submerging his body. The agony was unspeakable. He would have screamed but to open his mouth would only have increased the pain. He felt his soft underbelly blister and harden. He swam down, feeling like he was being deep-fried. *Crispy-fried dragon*, he thought.

It was too much. He turned around and tried to swim back up but he felt disorientated. He no longer knew which way was up. The more he swam the hotter he got. Even through his eyelids, the light was as intense as the heat. It was like swimming through the sun. *I'm going to die,* he thought. *Shute was wrong. This is going to kill me.*

His limbs gave up. He stopped moving. He was too tired. He had no energy. *So this is how it ends,* he thought. *My life ends where it began, in the fire of the Outer Core.* Dirk felt strangely calmed by this idea.

Then a voice that was not his own grew inside his

162

head, saying, *IT IS NOT YOUR TIME TO DIE YET*, and something grabbed him. He was too weak to fight it as it hauled him out of the liquid fire.

At last, he gasped for breath but his lungs were only filled with stale, hot, dry air.

'I think he's dead,' he heard a voice say.

Chapter Twenty-Two

Dirk opened his eyes to see an upside-down Sea Dragon peering at him.

'Oh no, hang on, he's alive,' she said.

Dirk felt so hot that he would have peeled off his own skin to cool down. He had a headache of epic proportions and he was exhausted.

'How many claws am I holding up?' said the Sea Dragon.

'Three,' said Dirk.

'What's your name?'

'Dirk Dilly.'

'What's your favourite food?'

'Baked beans,' replied Dirk.

'Yep, he's OK,' she said, moving back.

'Where am I?' asked Dirk.

'A human would call it hell,' said a male Shade-Hugger, stepping into view, lowering his brown head to get a closer look at him. 'We dragons are more clinical in our descriptions. Welcome to the Inner Core, friend.' There was something familiar about his face – something in the eyes.

Dirk took in his surroundings. The solid surface he stood on was translucent like frosted glass and full of huge holes. Below, the Outer Core bubbled and hissed angrily. Above and all around were more interlinking chambers, creating a matrix of interconnected caves that resembled a giant beehive.

'Here, have some water,' said the Shade-Hugger, offering Dirk a black metal flask. Dirk noticed that both his and the Sea Dragon's skin were covered in severe burn marks.

He took the flask and unscrewed the top but as soon as air hit the water it turned to steam.

The Shade-Hugger and Sea Dragon laughed.

'Sorry, I should have warned you,' said the Shade-Hugger. 'We're all out of ice down here.'

'The trick is to knock it back quickly,' said the Sea Dragon, handing him another.

165

This time Dirk managed to feel a couple of droplets on his tongue before it vaporised.

'Who are you?' he said.

'This is Almaz Bartosz,' said the Shade-Hugger, introducing the Sea Dragon. 'My name is Elsinor Cuddlums.'

'You're Karny's brother,' said Dirk.

'You know Karnataka?' said Elsinor.

'Yeah, he's an old friend. He's mentioned you. You were the one who attacked a Romanian village,' said Dirk.

'That's what I was convicted of, certainly,' he said, with a bitter laugh. 'I've never even been to Romania. There are many guilty dragons down here but we who are innocent stick together.'

'What's your story?' Dirk asked Almaz.

'Another Sea Dragon called Salt Sheasby accused me of being a Kinghorn,' she replied, 'just so she could steal my seaweed farm. If I ever see her again, I'll tear her apart.'

'And what about you, Mountain Dragon?' said Elsinor. 'Are you guilty of your crime?'

HE HAS NOT BEEN BANISHED. HE CAME HERE OF HIS OWN FREE WILL.

Dirk felt the words in his head. He turned round. At

first all he could make out were two yellow circles, even brighter than everything else. Then the circles vanished and reappeared in what Dirk realised was a blink. The two enormous eyes were set into a dragon's face, bigger than any he had ever seen. He didn't need to ask her name. He recognised the voice. It hadn't changed in the thousand years since the last time he had heard it at the conference in the Himalayas.

'Minertia,' he said, bowing his head. It was her voice he had heard in the liquid fire.

'Minertia found you in the Outer Core,' said Elsinor. 'She told us where you were and we hauled you in.'

YOU COME SEEKING THE TURNING STONE. Minertia spoke in Dirk's head but he could tell the others could hear too.

'I want to hide it. Others are seeking it,' said Dirk.

IT WILL NOT BE FOUND.

Minertia's words felt reassuring. Dirk knew with certainty that she was right. Wherever it was, the Turning Stone was out of Vainclaw's reach.

As he thought this, the ground shook. Dense black smoke poured from Minertia's nostrils.

VAINCLAW GRANDIN . . . CROWLEY'S SON. IT WAS HE WHO HAD ME SENT HERE.

Dirk looked into the ancient dragon's enormous eyes.

'Why don't you come back with me?' he said. He turned to the others. 'All of you. The Firedrake is expecting a dip in the temperature when I return. You'll be able to get out of this place. Elsinor, your brother is captain of Dragnet. He has the power to give you all reprieves. After all you said yourself, you're all innocent.'

'Karnataka? Captain?' said Elsinor.

'You mean we could be free once more?' said Almaz.

WHAT OF ME? I AM GUILTY OF MY CRIME, said Minertia. *I BREACHED THE FORBIDDEN DIVIDE. I BROKE THE LAW THAT I CREATED.*

'But you never attacked humans, did you?' said Dirk.

NO, IN THE COUNCIL'S EYES IT WAS WORSE. I TRIED TO MAKE PEACE WITH HUMANS, BUT IT DOESN'T CHANGE THE FACT THAT I WAS RIGHTLY CONVICTED.

'We won't go without Minertia,' said Elsinor.

'That's right,' said Almaz.

'You won't get a chance like this again,' said Dirk.

I AM OLD. MY TIME IN THIS WORLD IS

168

NEARING AN END. I WOULD BARELY SUR-
VIVE THE SWIM, BUT YOU, ELSINOR AND
ALMAZ, ARE YOUNG. YOU SHOULD GO
WITH THE MOUNTAIN DRAGON AND GET
OUT.

'We won't leave you,' said Almaz.

'We will remain loyal to the end,' said Elsinor.

Minertia turned her eyes to look at the two dragons
stubbornly standing in front of her, their skin blackened, blistered and sore from life in the Inner Core.

ELSINOR, ALMAZ, I AM MOVED BY YOUR
LOYALTY BUT I CANNOT ALLOW YOU TO
PASS UP AN OPPORTUNITY LIKE THIS.

'We will not abandon you,' said Elsinor.

THEN WE SHALL GO TOGETHER.

Suddenly Dirk felt the ground beneath him shake.
Minertia was stamping her feet; the translucent ground
was cracking, crumbling into the liquid fire.

'What are you doing?' said Almaz.

WE HAVE LIVED LIKE THIS TOO LONG. LET
US GO TOGETHER.

Dirk saw Almaz, Elsinor and Minertia slip into the
liquid fire at the same time that he lost his footing and
plunged head first into the boiling liquid. Once again,
the intense pain almost knocked him out but he

managed to stay conscious. He tried to propel himself forward, but it was impossible to tell whether he was making any progress. Once again he felt that he would die in the infernal lake. Then Minertia's voice floated into his head, her words cooling his overheated brain.

THIS, MY LAST SECRET, I GIVE TO YOU AND YOU ALONE, DIRK DILLY. AT THE CONFERENCE IN THE HIMALAYAS TO DECIDE MANKIND'S FATE, WHEN I COUNTED THE VOTES THERE WERE MORE DRAGONS IN THE AIR THAN ON THE GROUND. BY RIGHTS, WE SHOULD HAVE GONE TO WAR. I LIED TO PREVENT THAT.

Why are you telling me *this?* Dirk thought.

BECAUSE SOMEONE NEEDS TO KNOW HOW DELICATELY BALANCED ARE THE SCALES BETWEEN WAR AND PEACE. SOMEONE WHO CARES.

The words vanished and the burning pain returned. Dirk felt a surge of energy. He swam harder and faster.

Eventually he felt his head break the surface of the fiery lake. He flapped his wings and shot from the Outer Core, flying over the lava lake to the shore. The thin material on his wings was scorched and painful. He collapsed on to his back, panting.

170

Almaz and Elsinor were already there, pacing back and forth.

'Where is she? Where's Minertia?' demanded Elsinor.

'I don't know,' replied Dirk. 'But you should get going. If anyone finds that you've escaped, they'll take you back.'

'We'll wait for Minertia,' said Elsinor.

'She'll be out in a minute,' said Almaz, watching the surface nervously.

Dirk didn't say what he felt – that there was no point waiting, that Minertia had told him her final secret because she knew all along she would die in the Outer Core.

Chapter Twenty-Three

H olly and Archie were having a great holiday. Yesterday they had walked down the star-paved street full of people dressed up as famous movie characters, and today Dad and Big Hair had driven them to the beach. Occasionally Holly would look at Archie and notice sadness in his eyes and she would remember about his mum, then Archie would make a joke or do something silly to make her laugh and they would get back to enjoying themselves. Real life could wait. This was too much fun.

When they got home, they got out of the car to see Miss Gilfeather walking briskly up the drive.

'I am sorry to bother you, Mr and Mrs Bigsby.'

'Not at all,' said Holly's dad. 'Miss . . . er . . .'

'Gilfeather,' said Holly.

'Please, call me Vivian,' she said. 'I wonder whether I could borrow Holly and Archie for a short while.'

Mr Bigsby said that would be fine and, as Miss Gilfeather led them down the drive, through the gates next door to Petal's house, Holly asked, 'What do you need us for?'

Miss Gilfeather stopped and spoke very quietly. 'It's Petal. She's terribly upset. Do you know, I actually feel sorry for her. Nothing I say helps. Her mother is incommunicado and none of her other friends are answering the phone. So I thought maybe you could talk to her.'

'But she hates us,' said Holly.

Miss Gilfeather looked at Holly then at Archie and smiled. 'Oh, I don't think so. In fact, in her own little obnoxious way, I think she's rather fond of you. But that isn't the point. The point is she is upset, and I am asking you to make her feel better.'

She took them inside and showed them into the lounge, where Petal was sitting on a sofa that was the shape of a pair of lips. Her face was blotchy and red from crying. In front of her was a TV screen, paused on a smiley-faced TV presenter with the words

Hollywood Gossip behind her.

Holly and Archie looked at each other then back at Petal.

'Hi, Petal,' said Archie.

'Leave me alone. This is a disaster,' she replied, waving a hand dismissively. 'It's not fair. It's not even true. They shouldn't be allowed to tell lies like that. Chase is coming over in a minute. He'll put things right.'

'Put what right? What's wrong?' asked Holly.

Petal pressed the play button on the remote control.

'. . . And now the latest gossip from Tinseltown, Hollywood,' said the presenter. 'Rumour has it that *Petal – The Movie*, the film version of Petal Moses' autobiography, is set to be a total flop.'

Behind her, an unflattering photo of Petal appeared. She was mid-blink and chewing gum. Seeing it, Petal howled in misery.

'Our spies on set say that Miss Moses is following in her mother's footsteps.' The presenter paused then added, 'She's an awful actress too. Hollywood legend Chase Lampton must be worried about the impact the film will have on his flagging career, not to mention that of his son, Dante. Mr Lampton refused to speak to our reporter.'

The picture of Petal was replaced by images of Chase quickly getting into the back of a car, being driven away.

'His silence speaks volumes,' continued the presenter. 'And, in spite of her executive producer status, Petal's oh-so-famous mother has been strangely distant from the project. Suspiciously, as her daughter's movie looks to become the biggest turkey this side of Christmas, her mum is off recording a new album. A case of *Don't blame me*, perhaps.'

Petal hit the pause button and the picture froze on the presenter's plastic smile.

'Wow!' said Archie.

Holly tried to think of something better to say. She wasn't exactly a fan of Petal but, seeing her so upset, she felt sorry for her.

'It's simply terrible,' said Petal.

'But these are just rumours,' said Holly. 'No one's even seen the film yet.'

'That's very true,' said Chase Lampton, staggering into the room, closely followed by Miss Gilfeather.

'Mr Lampton, I must insist you leave,' she said.

The director smelt strongly of alcohol.

'Now, Vivian,' he replied, 'I do wish you'd chase me call . . . no, that's not right. Call me Chase. That's it.'

'I'll do no such thing. Now come along, you are in no fit state.'

'I tell you what's in no fit state,' said Chase, flopping on to the sofa next to Petal. '*Petal – The Movie*. It's a piece of junk. One more flop, the studio said. This was my last chance and what have I done? I've taken a kids' film and made a disaster movie . . .' Chase fell back, laughing at his joke. Petal burst into tears.

Holly and Archie glanced at each other.

'Now, Mr Lampton,' Miss Gilfeather squawked, 'are you telling this twelve-year-old girl that the film she has spent all summer making is no good? Are you saying that after one bad report on some silly gossip show you're giving up on it? Is that what you're saying?'

Chase Lampton stopped laughing. He sat up straight. Her words seemed to have sobered him up. He looked at the floor and mumbled, 'No, Miss Gilfeather.'

'I'm sorry?' she said.

'It'll be fine.' Chase turned to Petal, who had stopped crying. 'It's just Hollywood rumours, Petal. It's going to be a great movie.'

'Really?' said Petal.

Chase stood up, avoiding eye contact with Petal. 'Yeah, of course. We'll put a great soundtrack on it, lots of quick cuts. It'll be great. And hey, it's the wrap party tomorrow night. I'll get Theo to invite everyone who's anyone. By the next morning everyone will be saying what a great movie it's going to be. People are easily distracted in Hollywood. You two must come,' he said, pointing at Archie and Holly. 'And, of course, you, Vivian. You'll save a dance for me, won't you?'

He tried to demonstrate this with a fancy dance step but lost his footing, tripped on a leopard–skin rug and fell over with a THUD.

'I think we'd better take you home,' said Miss Gilfeather, picking him off the floor and dragging him to the door. 'Come along.'

'See you all at the party tomorrow night,' said Chase.

'Blimey,' said Archie once he was gone. 'That was odd.'

'You see?' said Petal. 'I knew Chase would make it all better. The film will be great. I'll have to buy a new dress for the party, of course.'

'But –' Holly's protest was cut short by a nudge in the ribs from Archie.

'It's better than crying,' he muttered through his teeth. 'See you at the party, Petal,' he said out loud.

'I can't really see why you're invited. You were only

extras, after all,' she replied.

Archie yanked Holly out of the room before she could respond. Outside, Miss Gilfeather had just managed to shove Chase into the back of his car.

'How is she?' asked Miss Gilfeather.

'Back to normal,' replied Holly.

'Oh,' said Miss Gilfeather. 'Oh well, I suppose that's an improvement. Thank you.'

Chapter Twenty-Four

It was a long journey from the banks of the Outer Core to the surface but Dirk was glad to feel it getting cooler as he inspected his scorched belly in the diminishing orange glow of earthlight. It was blistered and blackened but it would heal more quickly than the terrible injuries Almaz and Elsinor had sustained during their exile.

He had left them on the beach waiting for Minertia to appear. He hadn't told them about her final confession. She had said the secret was just for him.

The rock pulled away above his head to reveal the early morning sky above. Dirk figured he must have been gone a couple of days. He was on a hill from which he could see the outskirts of Los Angeles. He headed down the hill and travelled across rooftops but every flap of his wings hurt, so he found a truck going in the right direction, jumped on top and blended with it.

The book on the history of Sands Hall had given Dirk an idea but he wanted to give his wounds a little time to heal before putting his plan into action. Still avoiding Kitelsky and Putz, he steered clear of the Hollywood sign and, instead, found the cinema across the road from Sorrentino Solutions, where he connected to the phone line.

'. . . I'm sorry, Mr Smith, Mr Sorrentino isn't in today,' Sandra was saying.

Dirk listened in to a few more calls but everyone got told the same thing. Sorrentino was out of town.

Only Mr Tanner, in amongst all the Mr Smiths, was told something different.

'Mr Sorrentino left a message for you,' said Sandra. 'He said to say that your problem will be solved tonight, sir.'

'I see. Thank you,' said Mr Tanner.

Dirk disconnected from the phone and went to find Hunter and Frank. It took him a while to locate the yellow van but eventually he found it parked outside a public library. Hunter was waiting beside it when Frank came running out, waving a piece of paper in the air, crying, 'Man, I've got it! I've found it!'

'Calm down, Frank. What are you talking about?' said Hunter.

'The Turning Stone,' replied Frank. 'I know where it is. Or at least I know where it was last seen. Look.'

Hunter took the piece of paper and read it then looked up at his colleague and said, 'What's this from?'

'It's a photocopy of an article published in the seventies.'

Hunter read aloud from the article. '"*The Stone was like a globe, perfectly smooth with a hole through the middle.*"'

'Sounds right, right? You seen who wrote it?' said Frank. 'And look what the article's called.'

'"*The Summit of Skull Rock*",' read Hunter. 'What is that?'

'I don't know but Buchanan's gonna like this,' replied Frank.

The two men got into the van and Dirk was about to follow when he felt a sharp pain in his tail.

He turned to see Kitelsky's claws around his tail, a bubbling noise coming from his throat.

'So, you go sneakin' off without us, disappear for

days, then we find you here, sittin' lollin' in the sun. This ain't no vacation, Dilly.'

'Yeah, we got scores to settle, Dilly,' said Putz, lifting his head above the sloping roof.

'You spike-headed idiots!' hissed Dirk angrily. 'I'm in the middle of the investigation.'

'Yeah, so what you found out, then?' said Kitelsky.

'The film was stolen by Mo Sorrentino,' he said.

'Mo?' said Putz.

'That's right. He runs a business in town, ruining people's lives. He was the one who sold the film.'

'That no-good double-crosser!' said Kitelsky.

'So where's the film now?' asked Putz.

'It's with a human called Brant Buchanan but there are more important things to deal with first. Have you heard of Skull Rock?'

'Sure. It's back in the desert,' said Kitelsky.

'I need you to take me there,' said Dirk.

'We'll take you there as soon as we have the film,' said Kitelsky.

'That's right,' said Putz.

Dirk growled. If they hadn't been in the middle of the city, he would have roared fire in their faces. Dirk thought fast. He needed to check whether Hunter and Frank were right about the Turning Stone but he also remembered how sure Minertia had sounded that it could not be found.

'OK, here's the deal,' he said. 'We'll go and get the film quickly then you take me to Skull Rock. OK?'

Kitelsky and Putz looked at each other and nodded.

'Let's go get it, Dilly,' said Kitelsky.

Chapter Twenty-Five

'Oh yes, I've already had lots of other roles offered,' Petal was saying to a circle of reporters. 'Except they're all for parts playing, well, little girls. My agent thinks it very important that I don't get stereotyped at this stage in my career. That's the problem with Hollywood – everyone wants to put you in a box.'

'I wish we could put her in a box,' said Archie.

'And post it to the moon,' added Holly.

The party was being held at World Studios on the set of Little Hope Village Hall. The wooden chairs had been cleared to one side and on the stage a jazz trio was playing far too quietly to be heard above the throng of people. Holly and Archie had spent a while trying to spot famous people, but the novelty soon wore off when most of them were 'that bloke from that thing about the big missile' or 'that woman who played an alien in that film about the world blowing up'.

'I'm starving,' said Archie. 'We need to find some of those waiters with the food trays.'

On their way across the room they saw Miss Gilfeather talking to Chase Lampton. Her auburn hair was down around her shoulders and she was wearing a black silk dress.

'Hello, Miss Gilfeather. You look nice,' said Holly.

'Thank you, Holly. I feel sorry for those poor musicians on stage. I can't hear a note they're playing with all these awful film people talking,' she replied. She turned to Chase, who had slid his sunglasses into the pocket of his black suit jacket. 'Now, Chase, I think you owe these two an apology.'

The director looked at them. 'I'm very sorry for my shameful appearance yesterday. I was tired and drunk and there was no excuse for my behaviour.' He looked at Miss Gilfeather. 'How was that?'

'Very good. Holly and Archie, I hope you accept Mr Lampton's apology.'

They said they did and Holly said, 'Petal seems to be back on form.'

'Shallow waters are easily calmed,' said Miss Gilfeather. 'Are you having a nice time?'

'Yes, thanks,' said Archie and Holly. 'We're off to find some food.'

'If you see my son on your travels, can you ask him to come find me? It's almost speech time,' said Chase, as a passing waiter topped up his and Miss Gilfeather's champagne glasses.

Holly and Archie continued through the crowd.

'There's Dante,' said Archie, 'talking to that boy.'

Holly looked and saw Dante in a corner talking excitedly to a boy with dark greasy hair. The boy raised a hand and smoothed down his hair, edging away from the director's son while nervously glancing around.

'It's Callum,' said Holly, making her way over.

'Who?' said Archie.

'Callum Thackley, the person Dante was supposed to be playing.'

'Crazy Callum Thackley? I've got to meet him,' said Archie, walking over.

'Don't call him that,' said Holly.

They reached the two boys and Callum's dark eyes flickered briefly to look at Holly. He edged away.

'Hey, guys,' said Dante, 'look who it is. I've been

working on my accent, not that it matters now we've wrapped, but I reckon I came pretty close, eh, Callum?'

Archie put out a hand but Callum let out a nervous giggle and shrank away. Dante laughed.

'I really wish we'd met before I did the film,' he said, imitating Callum's movements.

'Dante, your dad's looking for you. He said something about a speech,' said Holly.

'Right. I'll see you later, Callum,' Dante said, slapping him on the shoulder.

Callum tensed up, smoothed down his hair and looked at the floor.

'I love this guy,' said Dante, leaving to find his dad.

'How are you, Callum?' said Holly.

He edged closer, still avoiding her gaze, and spoke quickly, breathlessly. 'They say I'm making progress but only because I pretend that it's not true. I say I know the monsters are in my head because that's what they want to hear. I say I want to get better and I don't believe these things. But Callum lies. They are there, Holly knows. They are real, with real claws and real teeth and real flames and real anger. Soon everyone will know, won't they?'

Holly and Archie exchanged a glance.

'Has he been in contact again?'

Callum didn't respond.

'Vainclaw,' said Holly. 'Has he spoken to you recently?'

'Master is always there, in my head. He's always with me. Soon he'll come back for me.'

Something behind Holly made him stop talking. Holly and Archie turned round to find Brant Buchanan standing behind them.

'Ah. I was hoping you'd get a chance to meet my house guest,' he said.

'Callum's staying with you?' said Holly.

'His father is an old friend of mine,' said Mr Buchanan, 'and Callum's been through so much, I thought he deserved a holiday. You used to go to school together, didn't you? What an appropriate setting for a reunion.' He motioned to the film set. 'I expect it brings back all sorts of memories.'

'Excuse me, everyone,' a voice was saying through the microphone. The crowd fell quiet. Theo Leggett was standing on the stage, red-faced and nervously tapping his glass on the microphone. 'Hi. Thanks. Ladies and gentlemen, I'm proud to give you Chase Lampton, his son, Dante Lampton, and the leading lady herself, Petal Moses.'

The three of them walked on to the stage to applause. Petal was beaming with pride. Chase took the microphone. 'Thanks, Theo.' He addressed the crowd. 'My old man, Connor Lampton, used to say that making movies is like making a cake. All you need are the right ingredients, the right amount of time and a hungry audience. Well, for this particular cake we . . .'

The sound of a mobile phone ringing interrupted him.

'. . . I'm sorry, that's mine,' said Chase, laughing. 'I meant to turn it off. Just one second.' He pulled the phone from his jacket and answered it. 'Hi, I'm kind of busy right now,' he said, winking at the crowd. The audience laughed too but Chase's face suddenly fell. 'I see, right,' he said seriously, stepping back from the microphone, talking on the phone. For a moment no one was sure what to do. Petal and Dante stood grinning uncomfortably, glancing at Chase. The director returned to the microphone. 'Ladies and gentlemen, there is no need for alarm but I need you all to leave the building as calmly as you can. There is no danger, but I've been informed that a fire has started in another part of the studio.' A concerned hum rose up in the hall. Chase raised his voice over it and said, 'As I say, nothing to worry about but studio regulations require that all hangars must be evacuated. I'm sorry for the inconvenience.'

The crowd turned and made for the door. Buchanan placed a hand on Callum's shoulder and led him out.

'Why would Callum be staying with Buchanan?' said Holly as they shuffled out.

'It makes sense that he would know his dad. I mean, a man like Buchanan must know loads of important people,' said Archie.

'I suppose,' said Holly. 'But Buchanan's interested in dragons and Callum's been in contact with the most dangerous dragon of all. It's not good.'

Outside, the fire smelt like burning chemicals. Fire wardens in yellow bibs were showing everyone where to go. As they rounded a corner, they saw the blaze in a nearby building. Three fire engines had arrived and fire fighters were trying to keep it under control, while others were making sure that no one got too near.

Holly and Archie found Chase and Dante standing in the front row watching the flames. Dante turned round and looked at them. He looked upset and his voice trembled as he spoke. 'P . . . P . . . Petal's in there,' he said.

'What?' said Holly.

'Petal's over there talking to that woman who played someone in that thing about a giant octopus,' said Archie, indicating where Petal Moses was standing chatting to a vaguely familiar actress.

'Not her,' snapped Dante, 'the film. The whole film. It was all in there. It's all gone.'

'Gone?' said Holly and Archie together.

'That's right,' said Chase. 'They were duplicating the tapes when the place caught fire.'

Holly looked up at the director. Perhaps it was a trick of the light but she thought she saw the curve of a smile appear at the corners of his mouth. Then he spoke.

'You realise, Dante,' he said, 'that everything we worked for over these past few months has just gone up in smoke? Let's go get a bagel.'

Chapter Twenty-Six

'What is this place?' said Kitelsky.

'This is Sands Hall,' replied Dirk, slipping into tour-guide mode, 'built in 1924 as a retirement home for a former American president and designed by a famous architect. These trees were planted to keep the garden private.'

In order to guarantee the former president's privacy in his retirement the famous architect had planted rows of leafy trees at the back of the garden, which was where the three dragons were hiding from the hundreds of security cameras that had been installed to guarantee Brant Buchanan's privacy.

'What's this Blue-cannon want with a film of us,

anyway?' said Kitelsky.

'Buchanan,' corrected Dirk, 'and I don't know.'

'So why don't we just go get it?' said Putz, pushing forward.

Dirk blocked his way. 'Because we don't want your cameo turning into a leading role. The place is covered in security cameras.'

'How do we get the film without being seen, then?' asked Kitelsky.

'Simple,' said Dirk. 'We cut the power.'

From the book Archie had given him Dirk had learnt that the electricity supply to Sands Hall came in via a locally located substation, housed inside a small red-brick structure. Nothing in the book indicated that the building had a back-up generator.

Dirk pointed out the substation to Kitelsky and Putz.

'So we just need to trash and smash it,' said Putz, once again trying to edge forward.

'Wait,' said Dirk. 'There are cameras pointing at that too.'

'So what do you suggest?' said Kitelsky irritably.

'There's a vent on top, directly in the middle. I need one of you to spit poison through the vent. It should burn straight through the equipment and short the whole place. But you can't break your cover. You need to hit it from here.'

'That's impossible,' said Kitelsky.

'It's not impossible,' said Putz. 'We used to play target practice on that old rock up in Beggar's Canyon back home. That was about the same distance.'

'You think it's so easy, you do it,' said Kitelsky.

'OK. I will,' said Putz.

He looked at the target, took aim and tilted back his head. A bubbling noise came from his throat. Dirk and Kitelsky watched anxiously. Suddenly Putz made a gagging noise and a stream of fluorescent green liquid shot from his throat, flying through the air, arcing then heading down towards the substation.

But it overshot and hit a pot plant, melting straight through both the plant and the pot.

'Get out of the way. I'll do it,' said Kitelsky. 'I always was a better shot than you.'

'Don't go any further than the edge of the trees,' warned Dirk as Kitelsky crept forward and took aim. Kitelsky did the same as Putz only this time the poison was right on target.

There was an electrical fizzing followed by a loud CRACK! and every light in and around the mansion went out, including the little red lights on the security cameras.

'Good shot,' said Dirk. 'Now stay here.'

'We're comin' wi' you,' said Kitelsky.

'Yeah, that's right, wi' you,' said Putz.

'Listen, I haven't got time for this. There may still be humans in there and, if so, they're going to come running out, looking to find out what the problem is,' said Dirk, 'and we don't want them to find that the problem is a bunch of dragons creeping around. Now, stay here.'

He spread his wings and flew over the garden. His wings still hurt a lot. He landed on top of the cylindrical building, careful to avoid the glass roof. He was relieved to see no one rushing out to find out what was going on. It looked like the place really was empty.

He licked his left paw and stuck it on to the glass, then extended a claw on his right and carefully cut a circular hole, which he lifted away and slid to one side. He dropped into the moonlit room. With the electricity off he could clearly see the TV screen that Holly and Archie had described. He reached up and felt around the side, trying to locate a wire.

'You found it yet?' said a voice above him.

Dirk glanced up and saw Kitelsky standing on the glass roof, his spiky head peeking through the hole.

195

'I told you to stay back,' said Dirk.

'Relax, there ain't no one here,' he said.

'Yeah, relax, we're being careful,' said Putz, landing on the glass, which began to show signs of strain under the weight of the two dragons on it.

'Get off the glass, you idiots,' said Dirk.

The glass creaked as a crack snaked across it like a slow-motion lightning bolt.

'Hey, that ain't very friendly,' said Putz.

'It's not strong enough to support two –'

Dirk's words were cut short by the sound of glass shattering. He ducked and covered his eyes to protect them from the shards of glass that were raining down. Along with the glass came the two Desert Dragons, landing on top of him, their spikes jabbing painfully into his skin. The sound of tinkling glass lingered in the air for a few seconds then the room fell silent.

'Get off me,' snarled Dirk, white smoke billowing from his nostrils.

Kitelsky and Putz climbed off and stood back. Dirk stood up and shook the bits of glass off his back.

'Watch it! You almost got me in the eye,' said Kitelsky.

Dirk flew across the room, grabbing Kitelsky and slamming him into a wall of books that fell down, whacking them both on the head.

'Listen, you no-good desert rat,' said Dirk. 'It's your necks I'm trying to save here.'

'What are all these things?' said Putz, picking up a fallen book.

'They're called books,' said Dirk, releasing Kitelsky and snatching the book off Putz. 'Now stay back while I try to find the film.'

He returned to the TV screen and groped around until he found a black wire running behind the shelves. He followed it down, knocking away the books as he did so, until he came to one that wouldn't budge. He stooped down and inspected it. On its spine was the author's name, David Player. Dirk tapped it with his claw. It made a tink-tink noise. He felt along its spine and found an opening. He dug his claw in and forced a hidden drawer open. There was a disk inside. He went to take the disk, but the drawer shut again and part of the author's name lit up in blue, spelling DVD Player.

'Hey, that's us,' said Kitelsky.

Dirk spun round. On the screen was the film of the two Desert Dragons.

'I never seen myself before. I got some good moves,' said Putz.

'How can it be playing when we've cut the pow—' Dirk started. 'Quick, get out!'

But as he spoke sheets of metal shot up in front of the bookshelves. More metal moved across the floor, knocking the dragons off their feet. The same happened over the top, blocking out the moonlight. It all happened too quickly to get out. Dirk flicked out his claws and rammed them into the wall of metal, tearing a hole, but as he did so the metal he had ripped away re-formed. He tried again but the same thing happened.

'What's going on?' said Kitelsky.

'Help me,' said Dirk.

All three dragons went to work on the walls with teeth and claws but each time they tore a piece open it sealed itself before they could make the hole any bigger. A voice behind them caused them to stop.

'Welcome,' it said.

They looked up at the screen, where the voice had come from. The image of the desert had been replaced by a silver-haired man. Brant Buchanan smiled.

'I am sorry that I'm not here to greet you personally,' said the pre-recorded image, 'but rest assured I will be with you very shortly. In the meantime, please enjoy this short feature.'

'What's going on?' said Kitelsky.

Buchanan's image was replaced by footage of the inside of an office. Dirk recognised it at once. It cut to a different angle, then another, and then the screen split into three so he could see three alternative viewpoints.

'Hey, that looks like you, Dilly,' said Putz.

Dirk watched with dismay as he saw himself drop into the office, look around, reach up and help Holly in.

'A human,' said Kitelsky. 'Why, you double-crossin' no-good dragon!'

'I think you're trying to save your own scaly neck too from now on,' said Putz.

Chapter Twenty-Seven

When Petal learnt about the film being destroyed, she let out a piercing scream, cried, 'Someone's to blame,' then phoned her mum, who told her what to do.

'I have to take her for an emergency meeting with her lawyer,' Miss Gilfeather told Holly and Archie, rolling her eyes. 'Mr Buchanan has kindly offered to take you home.'

In the back of Brant Buchanan's luxury Bentley, the billionaire sat facing backwards, to the side of the plasma TV screen, opposite Holly, Archie and Callum.

'Poor Petal, all that work for nothing,' said Holly.

'Stupid girl with her stupid film, her life story destroyed, nothing left, all gone,' said Callum, smoothing down his hair.

Something beeped and Mr Buchanan pulled out a mobile phone from his pocket. He read the message on it and smiled. 'Ah, excellent timing. Excuse me.' He made a phone call. 'Hunter,' he said, 'meet me at Sands Hall. You can give me the information you're so excited about and I've got something to show you . . . Yes, see you shortly.' He pressed the disconnect button and looked at Holly. 'Now, if you don't mind, there's something I'd like to show you at the mansion before I take you home.'

'What is it?' asked Holly suspiciously.

Mr Buchanan's grey eyes sparkled with excitement. 'Have you ever played poker, Holly? No, of course, you're too young,' he said. 'There's an expression in the game, "to show one's hand". It means that all the players reveal what they're holding. No more bluffing, no more bets. It normally indicates the end of the game. Well, Holly Bigsby, our little game is also coming to an end. I think it's time to show our hands.'

'What are you talking about?' she said, trying not to look at Archie.

'I mean, no more secrets, Holly,' said Mr Buchanan.

'He knows. He knows about the monsters,' said Callum. 'He knows the truth.'

'What are you talking about?' said Holly, trying to laugh it off.

'I said no more bluffing,' snapped Buchanan, pressing a button, causing the screen to flicker to life. 'Now let me show you a little film that *I've* made. It's low budget and the camera work is a little shaky in places but it's got a terrific plot and I think you'll warm to the actors.'

Holly gasped. On the screen she and Dirk were breaking into Brant Buchanan's laboratory.

'The monster,' said Callum, seeing Dirk. He looked away, fidgeting nervously and smoothing down his hair.

The shot cut to Holly and Archie standing in the cylindrical library. '*But didn't he say that it was full of expensive books? Why wouldn't he have cameras?*' said Archie on the screen.

'That would be madness,' said Buchanan.

On the TV, Archie looked up at the film of the two Desert Dragons. '*But where's the actual film?*' said the onscreen Holly.

'You were watching a duplicated DVD,' Brant Buchanan answered her. 'You see, unlike World

Studios, I am more cautious with my films. This is my favourite bit now.'

The shot changed again, this time showing the exterior of a house. It was dark and the camera zoomed in to find Holly and Archie standing on a balcony. Archie held up a book. A tail materialised from something on the roof and took it.

'I believe it's called blending, a skill unique to the Mountain Dragon,' said Mr Buchanan.

They heard Dirk say, '. . . *my gut tells me that anyone as wealthy as Buchanan is going to want to keep a secret like this to himself for a while.*'

'How very astute,' said Mr Buchanan. 'The phone's tapped, of course.'

Holly felt dizzy. Her hands were shaking but she felt Archie take one of them and grip it tightly.

'You'll never find him. No one will believe you,' Archie said firmly. 'People will say you faked this with special effects, that you're a mad rich man with too much time on your hands. You'll end up a gibbering wreck like Callum with monsters in your head.'

'The monsters are crawling out of my head,' said Callum.

'I have no interest in letting everyone in on our secret, Mr Snellgrove. Not yet,' said Buchanan.

'Then what do you want?' said Holly.

'Want?' said Buchanan, as though seeing how the word tasted in his mouth. 'For years I haven't *wanted* for anything. I did or I had. I never wanted. And then you appeared with your dragon friend and gave me something new to *want*.' He leant forward. 'I want a dragon. I want your dragon.'

'You'll never catch him,' said Holly.

'Ah, but thanks to you I already have,' said Buchanan. 'When you called Mr Dilly about the missing film, it gave me the idea. I knew that the only way for him to retrieve it from the library would be to cut the electricity supply at the substation but, you see, what the history book you gave Mr Dilly didn't mention was that I have recently installed a back-up generator. Tonight, while we were at the party, the power went off and the generator kicked in. Do you know what that means? It means that awaiting us is a real, live fire-breathing dragon.'

'He'll escape. Dragon claws can cut through anything,' said Holly.

'As you proved when you cut through the hole in my laboratory roof,' said Buchanan, pressing a button in the armrest and skipping back to the footage of Dirk and Holly in the laboratory. On the film Holly had just run back into the room and she and Dirk were hiding.

Holly was relieved to see that she was not in vision when she blended with the sofa. At least that secret remained intact.

'The challenge was how to hold a creature that can tear through anything. Tricky. It was Weaver who came up with the answer. What's that stuff called again?'

'IMM, Intelligent Memory Metal,' said Weaver, his voice coming through a speaker.

'Ah yes, that's it. Intelligent Memory Metal. Amazing stuff. It's as strong as titanium but it instantly re-forms when broken,' said Buchanan. 'I believe NAPOW created it for military use but so far no army has been able to afford it. I, on the other hand, had a little loose change, so I had it installed in the library. I'll be intrigued to see how Mr Dilly is dealing with it.'

Callum, whose eyes had been drawn to the screen, suddenly squealed and glanced at Holly. 'I remember him. At Little Hope. He made my master go away.'

'Vainclaw isn't your master,' said Holly.

'Vainclaw Grandin,' said Buchanan. 'Yes, he sounds like a fascinating character.'

Holly felt utterly defeated. Brant Buchanan knew everything and it was her fault. 'Why?' she said quietly.

Buchanan pressed a button, which produced a glass of whisky by his side. He took a sip and spoke. 'Let me tell you the secret to a successful business empire. Keep one step ahead of your competitors. If you know something they don't, you are stronger than they are. I'm already strong. I already know more than most. Imagine the strength this knowledge will give me.'

Weaver turned the car right, taking them up the driveway that led to Sands Mansion. They passed another car going down the hill. It was black with blacked-out windows.

'Who is that?' asked Buchanan.

'Probably just a lost tourist who saw the gates and turned around,' said Weaver.

The gates buzzed open and Weaver parked in the empty car park.

'Let's go and see the catch of the day,' said Mr Buchanan.

They stepped out of the car as the yellow VW van parked next to them.

'Hey, Buchanan, man,' said one of the long-haired men inside the van.

'How you doing?' said the other.

'Good evening, Hunter. Hello, Frank,' said Mr Buchanan.

'Looks like you're throwing a kids' party, man,' said Frank.

'If I was, I'd know where to find the clowns,' replied Buchanan. He turned to Holly. 'Frank and Hunter have been on a fact-finding mission for me. They suggested that Callum might be a useful house guest. His father was more than happy to let him visit, wasn't he, Callum?'

'Dad is scared of Callum,' said Callum. 'He can't remember what happened at the concert but he remembers the fear. I see it in his eyes.'

'Yeah, the concert,' said Frank. 'No footage, no one remembering anything — that concert was a classic cover-up, man.'

'But forget that. Now we got something really juicy, man,' said Hunter.

'All in good time,' said Brant Buchanan, leading them through the garden, down the steps and around the corner to the library, which was surrounded by scaffolding. Weaver pulled away the tarpaulin and opened the door to reveal a sheet of metal behind it.

'You see?' said Mr Buchanan, tapping the metal.

Callum was jabbering madly. 'They're in there. They're in there. The monsters are in there.'

'First contact with a real dragon, man,' said Frank.

'Weaver, open it up, then,' said Buchanan.

'Are you sure that's wise?' said Weaver.

Buchanan placed a hand firmly on Holly's shoulder. 'Oh yes, I think we'll be OK, don't you, Holly?'

Weaver reached into his jacket pocket and pulled out a small handgun. With his left hand he pressed a button on the side of the door and the metal sheet disappeared into the ground.

He stood back, keeping the gun levelled at the doorway.

The room was dark inside.

'You can come out now, Mr Dilly,' called Mr Buchanan.

They waited.

Nothing happened.

'Weaver,' said Mr Buchanan, looking at him.

Weaver nodded and, with his finger twitching on the trigger of the gun, stepped into the library. He switched the light on.

'Well?' said the billionaire. 'What have we got?'

'There's nothing here, sir,' said Weaver, stepping out. 'The top has been opened. It's escaped.'

Stuck inside the giant tin can, awaiting whatever fate lay outside, Dirk felt like a baked bean, which reminded him that, on top of being tricked, trapped and set up he was also starving.

'You've led us into a fine old mess, Dilly,' said Kitelsky, pacing around the circular room.

'It ain't his fault,' said Putz. 'We followed him here.'

'Either way, I'm itching to rumble and I got a hankerin' to rumble wi' Dirk Dilly, the dirty double-crossin' dragon detective,' said Kitelsky, skulking towards Dirk.

Dirk shot a line of fire at him, causing Kitelsky to yelp in pain. 'It's a shame you've used up your poison, then, isn't it?' snarled Dirk. 'Back off, Kitelsky.'

The three trapped dragons stared at each other.

'What's that on your nose?' said Dirk, noticing that the end of Putz's nose was illuminated as though a torch was shining on it from above.

'I don't know,' said Putz, trying to look at it and going cross-eyed in the process.

Dirk looked up and saw that the metal ceiling was retracting, revealing the night sky above. Moonlight was, once more, spilling into the room.

'What's going on?' said Putz.

'Come on,' said Dirk. 'Follow me.'

One painful flap of his aching wings was enough to get him to the rim of the building, where he could see that the grounds were floodlit and the security cameras were back on. One swivelled on its stick to point at him. Dirk sent an angry burst of fire at it, causing it to instantly blow up, and reducing it to a blackened crisp. Something caught his eye in the car park. In a dark shadow was a black car with blackened windows. A dark figure got in and slammed the door shut. It was too far away to make out his features. All Dirk saw was the wide-brimmed hat he wore. The engine started and the car drove away.

Kitelsky and Putz joined him on top of the building.

'What happened?' said Kitelsky.

'I don't know,' said Dirk.

'What now?' said Putz.

The sound of another car engine was approaching.

'We get out of here. Buchanan will have to wait,' said Dirk. 'Take me to Skull Rock.'

Chapter Twenty-Eight

As the dragons left the library, there was no avoiding being caught on camera, but Dirk knew he would have to worry about that later. The Turning Stone was more important right now.

They headed across the rooftops, out of town.

'Which way is Skull Rock?' said Dirk as they left the city lights behind them and entered the dark desert. Scraggy plant life caught on Dirk's claws and dragged along behind him. He shook his leg free and wished he was fit to fly but his wings still throbbed from his dip in the Outer Core.

'This way. It's on neutral territory,' said Kitelsky. 'It stands between all of our territories. It's where the three of us used to scuffle back when Mo was still out here.'

'Why all the interest in Skull Rock again, anyway?' asked Putz.

'What do you mean again?' replied Dirk.

'It was around thirty years ago when the Dragnet came sniffing around asking about Minertia,' said Kitelsky.

'Minertia?' said Dirk.

'Sure,' replied Kitelsky. 'That's where she breached the forbidden divide. We never saw nothing though, did we, Putz?'

'Not a thing,' said Putz.

'And you never saw the Turning Stone?' said Dirk.

'The Turning Stone?' said Kitelsky. 'So that's what this is all about. No, we never saw that.'

Dirk looked up at the sky. The moon was full and the stars seemed much brighter than they ever did in London. After they had been travelling a while, Kitelsky said, 'Skull Rock's just past that ridge.'

Dirk saw the pile of huge boulders he was pointing at rising high on the horizon. They drew nearer and scaled the stacked rocks, until they reached the top.

'Keep down,' said Dirk. In front of them was a large

rock shaped roughly like a human skull. At its base were two dragons.

'Kinghorns,' said Dirk. 'The Mountain Dragon's called Jegsy. The Sea Dragon is Flotsam. They work for Vainclaw.'

The two Kinghorns were using their claws to scratch away at the dirt, digging holes. 'They must be searching for the Turning Stone,' said Dirk.

'Well, if they think they can come strolling into our desert, scratching around, they've got another think comin',' said Kitelsky, standing up. 'You ready to rumble, Putz?'

'I sure am,' said Putz.

'No,' said Dirk, but it was no use. The two Desert Dragons had already spread their wings, splayed their spikes and flown down the hill, Kitelsky landing on Flotsam's back, Putz whacking Jegsy in the face. Bursts of fire shot from the Kinghorns' mouths. Putz and Kitelsky dodged the flames and went at them again, fighting with claws and teeth.

'Idiots,' said Dirk, shaking his head, staying at a safe distance.

A bubbling noise behind him caused him to spin round.

'Today I got no confusion. Today I know I got

poison, so no funny business, Dirk Dilly,' said Mo Sorrentino.

Dark grey smoke billowed from Dirk's nostrils but he didn't move, having no desire to be on the receiving end of a faceful of Desert Dragon poison.

'Where is he?' said Dirk.

'Who's the who you're referring to?' replied Sorrentino.

'Don't play games with me, Sorrentino,' said Dirk. 'You know who I mean – Vainclaw. I know those two are Kinghorns. I know Vainclaw's looking for the Turning Stone. I know that it was last seen out here with Minertia and I know that you aren't going to find it.'

'He seems to know a lot, this one,' said a low voice. 'Perhaps I should have employed him rather than you, Mr Sorrentino.'

From behind a rock stepped a dragon who at first looked like a moving shadow, but, as he stepped into the moonlight, he revealed his yellow belly.

'Fairfax Nordstrum,' said Dirk, instantly recognising the yellow-bellied, coal-black Cave Dweller that he had helped escape from the Dragnet cell.

'Dirk Dilly, the dragon detective. What brings you to the desert this evening?' replied Fairfax.

'So you're working for Vainclaw too?' said Dirk.

Fairfax smiled then slunk towards Dirk. 'Come, let's join the others,' he said.

'One move I don't like and you'll feel my poison, Dilly,' said Sorrentino, remaining behind him as Fairfax led him down the hill to where Kitelsky and Putz had been clamped down by the Kinghorns.

'Get yourself off of me,' said Kitelsky.

'Eh, Jegsy, I got spikes in my belly, like,' said Flotsam.

'They're a prickly pair, ain't they?' said Jegsy, ramming Putz's head against the ground.

'Mo Sorrentino,' said Kitelsky. 'You double-crossin', no good . . .'

'It's nothing personal,' said Sorrentino. 'It's just business.'

'Be careful with our spiky friends,' said Fairfax. 'I'm sure these fine Desert Dragons will join us once we explain the situation.'

'What situation?' demanded Dirk.

'First things first,' replied Fairfax. 'What makes you so sure we won't find the Turning Stone?'

'I went to the Inner Core' replied Dirk. 'I spoke to Minertia. She told me it was safe. I believed her.'

Again, Fairfax laughed. 'You see, Sorrentino?' he said, prowling around Jegsy and Flotsam, who were still struggling to hold the Desert Dragons down. 'Now that's initiative.'

'I didn't need to ask. I know it's here,' replied Sorrentino sharply. 'She had it when she arrived but not when she left.'

'And yet it doesn't seem to be here now. Maybe I should employ Mr Dilly to help me achieve my goal.'

'I wouldn't take your gold, Nordstrum,' snarled Dirk.

'What about power? Come and join the One-Worlders and you will be powerful,' said Fairfax.

'One-Worlders,' said Dirk, remembering what Karnataka had said about the Kinghorn splinter group. 'So you're Vainclaw's challenger.'

'Vainclaw Grandin,' sneered Fairfax. 'That half-winged idiot will soon bow down before me.'

Jegsy looked up from his struggle with Putz. 'Never,' he said, leaping off the Desert Dragon on to Fairfax's back. 'Vainclaw is the true leader of the Kinghorns,' he said, sinking his teeth into Fairfax's neck. Fairfax howled and lashed out with his tail, sending Jegsy flying.

'What are you doing, you idiot?' I am your leader now,' said the Cave Dweller, thick green blood trickling from his neck.

'I don't think so,' said a thundering baritone voice from behind Dirk.

Dirk spun round to see three shapes come from the darkness. It was Vainclaw Grandin, smoke billowing from his nose, with the two Scavenger brothers, Leon and Mali, standing on either side of him.

'Eh, it's Mr Detective,' said Leon.

'So it is. Hey, Jegsy,' said Mali, nodding hello.

Chapter Twenty-Nine

Flotsam flew angrily at Jegsy, claws thrashing. 'You led Vainclaw here, didn't you, you fool?'

'You wanted to follow the Cave Dweller but I'm a Grandin. Vainclaw is my leader.' Jegsy shot a defensive burst of fire at him and shouted over to the Scavengers, 'Leon, Mali, lend us a hand, lads.'

'Come on, ar kid,' said Leon.

'I'm right with you, bro,' said Mali.

'Who's the fool now, Flotsam?' said Jegsy.

The Scavenger brothers approached Flotsam but Kitelsky and Putz landed in front of them, rose up on to their hind legs, extended their claws and made their spikes point outwards, threateningly.

'Calm down, boys,' said Leon. 'We got no problem with you. We just want to help our mate here.'

'You come wanderin' into our territory, acting all tough, and you think you can tell us what to do?' said Putz.

'And I don't know how you do things back home, but out here in the desert we fight dragon to dragon,' said Kitelsky.

'What do you say, ar kid?' said Leon. 'Shall we respect the local culture or what?'

'Yeah, let's snap off their spikes one by one,' replied Mali, lunging at Putz as Leon spun round, sweeping his tail across the ground, knocking Kitelsky off his feet, then diving at him. The Desert Dragons were quick and dodged the flames that the Scavengers sent their way. Behind them Jegsy and Flotsam continued to fight viciously, tearing and scratching each other.

Dirk stepped back to avoid getting drawn into the brawl and felt something spike his tail.

'I've still got my poison,' said Sorrentino.

'Aren't you going to help your friends?' said Dirk.

'I help whoever pays me,' replied Sorrentino.

Also staying out of the fight were Fairfax Nordstrum and Vainclaw Grandin, standing nose to nose, maintaining eye contact. Grey smoke poured from Vainclaw's nose, mingling in the air with Fairfax's yellow smoke.

'You remind me of your father,' said Fairfax calmly.

'I'm stronger than my father,' Vainclaw replied, spitting fire at him.

Fairfax held his ground, simply lowering his head and allowing the flames to lick over his back.

'Crowley was strong enough,' he replied. 'Loyalty was the characteristic he lacked.'

'Why should he have been loyal to you?'

'Not to me, to the principles we laid out when we formed the Kinghorn Alliance, before you had even broken your eggshell. There were only three of us then – your father, myself and the Sea Dragon, Nessun Crumb. We all had our reasons to hate humanity and we vowed to wipe every human being off this planet. Then Crowley set up his company in the human world, Gronkong Shinard. He had always spent too much time in the company of humans for my liking. The next thing I knew he no longer wanted to destroy mankind. He wanted to enslave it. He didn't understand that humans are too spirited to live as slaves, too rebellious, too troublesome. Their entire history has been one of war –'

'No, their history has been one of domination,'

interrupted Vainclaw. 'The strong control the weak. Well, we are strong. And you say they cannot be slaves, and yet they have enslaved one another for centuries.'

'The only way to restore harmony to the world is to wipe out humanity,' said Fairfax.

'Killing all humans would be like trying to stamp out every ant or to squash every fly. Impossible,' said Vainclaw.

'So you really are your father's son,' said Fairfax.

'My father is dead,' replied Vainclaw. 'It is I, Vainclaw Grandin, the first up-airer, who will lead all dragons to victory now.'

Fairfax's eyes narrowed. He took a breath then opened his mouth and sent black flames at Vainclaw. Dirk could feel the intense heat even from where he was standing. Vainclaw staggered back, his face blackened by the fire.

'You dare to steal my title,' snarled Fairfax. 'You were a mere youngling then. I was the leader of the Kinghorns, the leader of the One-Worlders. I am the true first up-airer. Only Minertia stood in my way.'

'And yet it was I who got rid of her in the end, after she broke the forbidden divide in this very spot,' said Vainclaw.

'Hold on,' said Dirk. 'If you saw Minertia breach the forbidden divide, you would have seen what she did with the Turning Stone.'

Vainclaw kept his eyes focused on Fairfax but he replied to Dirk. 'I may not have actually seen Minertia breach the forbidden divide but I had it on good authority from one who did. Isn't that right, Sorrentino?'

'I got nothing to say. I respect client confidentiality,' said Sorrentino.

Dirk turned on the Desert Dragon. 'And you took the gold that Vainclaw paid you and used it to set up your business,' he said.

'Everyone's got a right to earn a livin', haven't they?'

'You lowlife,' said Dirk, diving at Sorrentino, catching him off guard, knocking him over and clamping his jaw shut with his forearm.

'Get off him. He's working for me now,' said Fairfax, breathing black flames at Dirk, which seemed to rip through his skin and burn his bones. Dirk cried out and released Sorrentino.

'Now you're going to get it,' said Sorrentino threateningly.

'What's that behind you?' said Dirk.

'I've seen too many films to fall for that,' said Sorrentino.

'Eh, there's someone coming,' said Mali.

The other dragons had stopped fighting. In the darkness, two bright white lights were approaching, sending long spiky shadows from the twisted Joshua trees across the desert landscape.

'Humans,' said Flotsam.

'Shouldn't we leg it?' said Jegsy.

'Kinghorns, hold your ground,' said Vainclaw and Fairfax as one, then snarled at each other.

'The detective must have led them here,' said Sorrentino.

'More like you sold the information just like you sold the film,' said Dirk.

'It's of little consequence,' said Fairfax. 'We'll kill these humans and then settle our differences.'

'On that, at least, we are agreed,' replied Vainclaw.

'In the place where Minertia sealed her own fate we will seal the fate of the world,' said Fairfax. 'We will destroy these humans as a symbol of our intentions to take back this world for all of dragonkind.'

The car came to a standstill directly in front of them. The engine cut out but the lights remained on. In their dazzling glare it was impossible to make out the figure who stepped out of the right side door and made its way to the front, standing in front of the beam.

'Prepare to die, human,' said Vainclaw, skulking forward.

'Oh, when you get to my age that's one thing you have to be prepared for,' said an elderly lady's voice. 'My Ivor used to say that being scared of death is like being scared of cheesecake, because there's really no point. Mind you, he was a silly man.'

'Mrs Klingerflim?' said Dirk.

'Hello, Mr Dilly,' she said. 'Don't worry. I'm not here about the rent.'

Chapter Thirty

Dirk stared at his elderly landlady in disbelief. 'What are you doing here?' he asked.

'Skull Rock,' she sighed, looking up at the rock behind them. 'Do you know, I haven't been here since I came with Ivor thirty-odd years ago.'

Dirk remembered the photograph he had seen of Mrs Klingerflim and her late husband in front of the rock.

'Eh, boss, can we kill her?' said Leon.

'Yeah, let's rip her head off,' said Mali.

'What a way to speak in front of a lady,' said Mrs Klingerflim, as the Scavengers approached.

Dirk needed to distract them somehow. Mrs

Klingerflim may not have been scared but he didn't like the idea of watching the sweet old lady being torn apart.

'But if you were out here dragon-spotting with Ivor, who took the photo?' he asked, skirting around the two Kinghorns, putting himself in a position where, if need be, he could throw himself in front of Mrs Klingerflim.

Mrs Klingerflim smiled warmly. 'You are clever, Mr Dilly. You've guessed, haven't you?'

'And that scratch on the lens?' said Dirk.

'Well, she had very big claws. It's a wonder she could operate the camera at all.'

'Who? What are you talking about?' said Vainclaw.

'Minertia Tidfell,' said Mrs Klingerflim, her eyes widening behind her thick glasses. 'She was the biggest, oldest and wisest dragon of them all. We were out here to watch these lovely Desert Dragons. I used to love watching you play-fighting,' she said, waving at Putz and Kitelsky.

'Watchin' us?' said Kitelsky.

'Play-fightin'?' said Putz.

'Then on the third day we heard a voice. She spoke in our heads, I remember. We turned round and there she was, as big as a mountain. I shall never forget it.'

Mrs Klingerflim wiped a tear from her eye.

'So she approached you?' said Dirk.

'Yes, it turned out she'd been watching us for some time,' she said, 'checking we were the right sort of people.'

'The right sort of people for what?' said Vainclaw.

'A reconciliation,' replied Mrs Klingerflim. 'She believed that the time had come for dragons to come out of hiding. She told us she thought she had made a mistake at the conference only giving dragonkind a choice between hiding and fighting. She dreamt of a world where humans and dragons could live side by side.'

'Impossible,' said Vainclaw.

'We thought that was a splendid idea. We were young then, well, younger than now, at least. It was the early seventies. We thought we could change the world, help dragons come out of hiding and live in harmony with humans.'

The dragons stood captivated, listening to the old lady.

'The Summit of Skull Rock,' said Dirk.

'That's what Ivor called it in some silly article he wrote. He did like to make things sound grand. It was just the three of us having a natter, really.'

'What happened to the Turning Stone?' asked Sorrentino.

Mrs Klingerflim took her glasses off, wiped them and put them back on. 'I remember you,' she said, peering at the Desert Dragon. 'You saw us. Minertia called out to you to join us but you ran away.'

'She had the Turning Stone when she arrived but not when she left. Where did she hide it?' Sorrentino said.

'I'm afraid it's not anywhere any more,' said Mrs Klingerflim.

'What do you mean?' asked Vainclaw.

'She destroyed it,' replied the old lady.

'She destroyed it?' said Fairfax Nordstrum, speaking for the first time since Mrs Klingerflim had stepped out of the car, the yellow smoke from his nostrils darkening.

'Oh, you're a coal-black, yellow-bellied Cave Dweller, aren't you, dear?' she said, turning to look at him. 'You're the first one I've ever seen.'

'And I'll be the last. Why did she destroy it?' said Fairfax in a measured tone.

'She said that it could too easily end up with the wrong sort of dragon,' said Mrs Klingerflim. 'So she put it between her teeth and split it into pieces. I took one of the bits as a souvenir. It makes a lovely paper-weight.'

'And now we shall put you between our teeth and split you into pieces,' said Vainclaw.

'Eh, boss, the old girl's not alone,' said Mali, who had noticed something else in the darkness. Dirk turned to see that another set of headlights was approaching from across the desert.

After discovering the library empty, Brant Buchanan ordered Weaver to take Holly, Archie and Callum back to the car.

'I wonder how he got out,' whispered Holly.

'Do you think Weaver will take us home now?' said Archie.

'I don't know. Where are we going, Weaver?' asked Holly, as they reached the car.

Weaver, who had his back to them, ignored her question and said, 'Get in.'

'The monsters will destroy us all,' said Callum.

They waited in the car until Buchanan returned. He sat in the passenger seat next to Weaver and addressed them through the plasma TV screen.

'We're going on a little outing,' he said.

'It's late,' said Holly. 'My parents will be worried if you don't take us home.'

'I own your father,' said Mr Buchanan sharply. 'I pay his wages. I tell him what to do. I tell him where to go and I'll tell him what time to expect his daughter home.'

The screen went blank and Weaver started the engine.

'Try the doors,' said Archie.

They turned the handles but they were all locked. The car headed down the driveway, through the gates and turned left on to a road where they stopped at a set of traffic lights. A black and white police car stopped alongside them.

'Try to get their attention,' said Holly.

Holly and Archie banged on the window. 'Help, we're being kidnapped!' they screamed, but the two cops didn't seem to hear them.

Brant Buchanan's face reappeared on the screen. 'Kidnapping is rather melodramatic,' he said. 'Anyway, I'm afraid the car is completely soundproofed.'

Holly and Archie sat back in their seats.

'He knows about monsters,' said Callum, smoothing down his hair.

The car headed south down a fast-moving motorway, past rows of white wind-turbines that moved in a strangely hypnotic way. Out of the city they took a left and drove up a quieter, darker road, with empty landscape on either side, so dark that it made the night sky look pale in comparison. Holly and Archie tried pressing every button in the high-tech car but nothing worked. Callum remained huddled in a corner, with a look of wild mania in his eyes. The car turned right on to a bumpy track then cut across the desert itself. A glass panel above the TV screen allowed them to see ahead. Strangely shaped trees were silhouetted against the sky. As they passed a huge clump of rocks, they saw something else. It was another light.

'I can't make out what I'm looking at,' said Archie.

They got closer and it became clearer.

'Dragons,' said Holly.

'See anyone you recognise?' said Buchanan.

Holly didn't respond but Callum said, 'My master.'

'Isn't that Mrs Klin—' Archie was cut short by Holly putting her hand over his mouth, not wanting Brant Buchanan to learn any more than he already knew.

The car stopped in front of the incredible scene and, after a moment, Mr Buchanan and Weaver got out and walked forward. Buchanan spoke to the dragons but, locked in the soundproofed car, neither Holly nor Archie could hear what he was saying.

Chapter Thirty-One

Weaver shifted his gaze from the scene outside the car and turned to look at his boss.

'Are you sure about this?' he said.

Brant Buchanan's eyes remained fixed on the dragons. 'There's always a little risk in business,' he replied.

'Yes, sir, but still.'

Working for a man like Buchanan, Weaver was accustomed to hostile environments. You didn't get to Buchanan's position without making a few enemies on the way. In the past Weaver had dealt with bitter former employees, angry competitors put out of business by Global Sands, and even the occasional crook with a plan to kidnap his employer for the ransom. In every one of these instances Weaver had assessed the risk and executed the necessary measures to keep Mr Buchanan from harm.

In the current situation, being in the middle of the desert with an unidentified car, ten rather vicious-looking dragons and an elderly lady, he had already established that the safest thing to do would be to turn the car around and drive quickly away. Unfortunately, Buchanan had already ruled out that option.

Weaver reached into the panel in the door and pulled out a large black gun.

'Just to be on the safe side,' he said, checking the cartridge.

'Remember to aim for the stomachs. They have soft bellies,' said Buchanan.

'And lethal claws, razor-sharp teeth and the ability to breathe fire,' added Weaver.

Buchanan smiled and said, 'That too.'

They both stepped out of the car and slammed the doors behind them. Weaver walked in front of the headlights, making sure everyone could see the gun he was holding.

'Greetings,' said Mr Buchanan. 'Before we begin, I'd

like to point out that Weaver here is carrying the very latest in our new range of machine pistols. It's capable of shooting up to nine hundred rounds of ammunition per minute. It has a range of fifty metres. It's loaded with armour-piercing steel bullets. And he's not afraid to use it.'

'You had our attention at "machine pistol",' said a red and green dragon that Weaver recognised from the film of the laboratory.

'Dirk Dilly,' said Mr Buchanan. 'At last we meet in the flesh.' He turned to the darker Mountain Dragon. 'And would I be right in thinking that this is Callum's play pal, Vainclaw Grandin?'

Vainclaw rose up on to his hind legs angrily but, hearing a click from Weaver's gun, landed back on all fours and remained where he was. 'Soon you will only speak my name when begging for mercy, human,' he snarled.

'I dare say you're right,' said Buchanan. 'But while Weaver's holding the firearm, I ask that you listen to me.'

'You got firearms. We got fire mouths,' said Jegsy, stepping forward and opening his mouth.

Weaver swung his gun to point at him.

'Don't hurt them,' said Mrs Klingerflim, but

Weaver didn't hear her. He just felt her touch and instinctively raised his elbow sharply, knocking the old lady flying. She landed face down between the two cars.

'Mrs K!' said Dirk, diving forward to help her.

There was no response.

'Stand back!' shouted Weaver, nervously pointing the gun at Dirk now.

'She's an old woman,' said Dirk.

'I said stand back,' repeated Weaver.

'And I said no,' said Dirk, moving towards where Mrs Klingerflim was lying.

Weaver squeezed the trigger and opened fire. The sound filled the air and smoke rose up from the gun.

Weaver released the trigger and the smoke cleared.

Dirk Dilly lay slumped on the ground. Green blood seeped out, forming a pool on the dusty desert floor around where his body lay.

'Now, do I have your attention?' said Brant Buchanan.

'What have you got to say to us?' said Vainclaw, in his deep baritone.

'I've come to make a deal,' Buchanan replied.

'What sort of deal?' said Vainclaw.

Fairfax shook his head. 'Just like your father,' he said. 'True Kinghorns do not make deals with humans. They destroy them.'

'We will make them our slaves,' said Vainclaw.

The two dragons snarled at each other.

'Destroy, enslave,' said Buchanan. 'I offer a third option.'

'Speak,' said Vainclaw.

'The ultimate war is coming,' said Buchanan, 'but I say, why divide the world between dragons and humans when we can divide it between the strong and the weak, regardless of species?'

Much to Weaver's agitation his boss had walked up to the two dragons and was standing between them, as they listened to what he was saying. Weaver felt his finger itch on the trigger.

'And believe me,' continued Buchanan, 'I am strong. I have technology and weaponry that will ensure our victory. Together, having conquered all those who stand in our way, we will rule this planet, dragon and man united in strength.'

The two dragons looked at each other, sending clouds of black and yellow smoke into Buchanan's face.

'It's an interesting proposition,' said Vainclaw.

'Your father would have said the same thing,' scoffed Fairfax.

The two dragons pulled away to face each other, Buchanan still between them.

'Sir,' said Weaver worriedly.

'Don't worry, Weaver,' said Buchanan. 'We are in the process of negotiation.'

But Weaver was looking at the claws that both dragons had extended. He was watching the other dragons as they gathered round.

'You have been most persuasive,' said Vainclaw, edging nearer to Buchanan.

'Dragons have methods of persuasion too,' said Fairfax, moving his fearsome face close to Buchanan's.

'Both of you, stand back,' shouted Weaver.

'Relax, Weaver,' said Buchanan.

The dragons were too close to his boss to risk firing at them. The recoil on the gun made it difficult to be completely accurate. Stray bullets could easily hit Buchanan. So instead Weaver raised the gun and aimed above their heads. He pulled the trigger and, for a second time, streams of bullets shot into the air.

The idea was to scare them off, so he could grab his boss and get out of there but, as the smoke cleared for a second time, Weaver found that no one had moved.

In fact, no one was moving at all. Every one of the dragons, and Brant Buchanan, were standing exactly as they had been, frozen, with a faraway look in their eyes.

Chapter Thirty-Two

Locked inside the car, Holly and Archie had watched helplessly as Weaver knocked Mrs Klingerflim into the dark space between the cars.

'Dirk!' screamed Holly as he took a round of ammunition in the belly.

Callum sat huddled in a corner, repeating, 'My master, he's here,' over and over again.

'Shut up, Callum,' said Archie, but he wasn't listening.

'Look,' said Holly, noticing that while Buchanan had the full attention of the dragons, a door in the black car opened and a shadowy figure lifted Mrs

Klingerflim inside. The man's face was obscured by a wide-brimmed hat. He disappeared into the car, unseen, as Weaver fired the gun a second time.

Seeing that everyone had frozen, Holly said, 'One of them must have used Dragonsong.'

'But which one?' asked Archie. 'None of them are moving.'

'Except for Weaver,' said Holly, seeing him walk up to his boss and wave a hand in front of his face. 'We've got to get out. If only we could break the . . .' She stopped. 'Of course.' She reached inside her T-shirt and pulled out the dragon claw she wore around her neck. 'Dragon claws can cut through anything,' she said.

Holly jammed the claw into the door and levered at it. There was a crunch as the claw cut through the lock and the door swung open.

'My master. He's not moving,' said Callum, slipping out and running to Vainclaw's side. Holly and Archie rushed to Dirk's unmoving body and fell to their knees.

'Try and push him over,' said Holly but, as much as they tried, they couldn't move him.

'You want a hand?' said a voice behind them. Holly spun round to see a familiar weather-beaten face beneath a wide-brimmed hat. She couldn't think of a time she had been as pleased to see anyone. She hugged him then said, 'Archie, this is Ladbroke Blake, the detective I told you about.' She turned back to him and said, 'What are you doing here?'

'Let's get this dragon on his back first.'

Weaver, who had been trying to wake up Mr Buchanan, turned round and said, 'What's happened to him?'

'Never mind him, give me a hand,' snapped Ladbroke, staring Weaver directly in the face.

Together, Weaver and Ladbroke pushed Dirk on to his back.

'I'm sorry, Holly. It looks bad,' said Ladbroke.

Holly forced herself to look. There were three holes in Dirk's chest. She fell to her knees and collapsed into tears, her hands across his belly. 'Oh Dirk,' she cried. 'Please say something.'

'I'm sorry,' said Weaver quietly.

Holly didn't register his words. She felt Dirk's blood fill the gaps between her fingers. She raised her head, looking at the stars, blurry through her teary eyes. This was the end, she thought. He was dead. Dirk was dead. Nothing meant anything any more. After all she had been through with Dirk, protecting mankind from the

Kinghorns, it was a human weapon that had killed him.

Killed.

Dead.

The words lost their meanings as Holly wept.

The pain in her heart was so overwhelming that she barely noticed the dull ache in her leg. But it was insistent. It came from the bone fixed by the Sky Dragon, Nebula Colorado. It felt as if the bone was trying to tell her something.

She remembered Nebula's words – *Part of me is now a part of you* – and suddenly she knew what to do. She didn't know how. She hadn't heard a voice or seen a vision. She simply knew as though she had always known.

'All of you, hold him down,' she said, wiping her eyes, smearing green blood across her cheek.

'Holly, he's dead,' said Ladbroke gently.

'Hold him down,' repeated Holly. 'You too, Weaver.'

'What's happened to Mr Buchanan?' said Weaver.

'Put the gun down and do as she says,' shouted Archie.

Weaver looked like he wanted to say something but he placed the gun on the ground, sat down and held

Dirk's tail. Ladbroke took his head and Archie held his wings. Callum remained where he was, stroking Vainclaw's paw and muttering, 'My monster, my master.'

Holly placed her hands over the gash where the bullet had gone in and concentrated. She sensed the torn flesh and the open arteries. Then she sensed the metal of the bullet itself. She focused hard and felt warming energy spread from her leg and fill her body. In her mind's eye she could see the bullet lodged inside the bloody mess. She focused on it, hooking it with her thoughts and drawing it out. Her hands remained still, but she could feel the bullet climbing back to the surface until she felt its cold metal in her palm. She closed her hand around it then allowed it to fall to the ground. With the bullet out, she placed her hands back on the wound and channelled the energy from the bone in her leg. By the time she had removed her palms, the wound had healed over.

'How did you do that?' Archie said.

'I don't know,' she said. 'But I've got to do the others quickly.'

As she retrieved the second bullet, Dirk's body twitched.

'Hold him down, make sure he doesn't injure himself,' said Ladbroke.

By the time Holly had extracted the third bullet and healed the final wound Dirk let out a low moan.

Chapter Thirty-Three

Dirk had once seen a TV show in which people described their near-death experiences. Most of them had described seeing tunnels with white lights at the end. As Dirk felt the bullets do their terrible work and his life force ebb away, he hadn't seen anything, but in the darkness he had heard something. At first it was just garbled noise, then he heard a voice he hadn't heard for a long time. It was his mother. He could hear the first words she had ever spoken to him, the first words he had ever heard, as he crawled from the Outer Core as a youngling. At the time he had been too young to understand but now as the words came back he heard her say, '*There, there, little one, you have finished the hardest journey.*' The voice grew fainter and he heard another. It was Minertia. '*Because someone needs to know how delicately balanced are the scales between war and peace,*' she said, '*someone who cares.*' He heard more voices, speaking over each over, garbled, growing louder and louder like an orchestra of noise.

The voices disappeared and suddenly there was silence – peaceful, endless silence – and Dirk knew that this was the end. This was death.

Then, in the dark nothingness, one more voice spoke.

'Dirk, come back to me,' said Holly, throwing her arms around him.

Dirk opened his eyes and raised his head. 'What happened?' he said.

'You swallowed a little lead,' said a man in a wide-brimmed hat.

'Ladbroke Blake?' said Dirk, lifting himself up and examining his blood-smeared belly.

'Dirk Dilly,' replied the craggy-faced man, smiling.

'It was you that rescued us from the library,' he said, 'but how . . .'

'Enough,' said Weaver, picking up his gun and jumping to his feet. 'What is wrong with Mr Buchanan?'

'The same thing that's wrong with all of them,' said Dirk. 'They're under the spell of Dragonsong.'

'But whose?' said Holly.

'I don't know,' said Dirk.

'As far as I could tell from the car,' said Ladbroke, 'both dragons sang at the same time.'

'They must have done it at precisely the same time and entranced each other as well as everyone else,' said Dirk.

'But how do we get him out of it?' asked Weaver.

'Like this,' said Ladbroke, slapping Mr Buchanan hard in his face. The billionaire rocked with the force of the slap. He blinked then he looked at Weaver with a vacant smile.

'Mr Buchanan, sir,' Weaver said, 'are you all right?'

'The monsters and the music. Did you hear the music? It sounded for ever. Did you see the monsters? They've gone now but they were here.'

'What are you talking about, sir?' said Weaver. 'What's wrong with him?'

'I don't know,' said Ladbroke. 'That should have worked.'

'Pretty music in my head and monsters in my hair,'

sang Brant Buchanan, ruffling his silver hair.

Dirk approached but Buchanan stared straight through him and said, 'All the monsters have gone now.'

Dirk lifted a paw and slapped him again.

Buchanan swayed and said, 'Where did the music go? Did the monsters take it with them?'

'It's like he's still under,' said Holly.

'Look at the positioning,' said Dirk. 'Vainclaw and Fairfax were on either side of Buchanan. They must have sung at the same time, wanting to get in first. Buchanan was directly in between both Dragonsongs. He got a double dose. It must have damaged his brain in some way.'

'Is there a cure?' said Weaver.

'I don't know. I've never heard of it before,' said Dirk. 'Why didn't it affect you?'

'Because he's deaf,' said Ladbroke.

'Deaf?' said Archie.

'But you can hear us?' said Holly.

'I lip-read,' said Weaver. 'I have done all my life. It's trickier with dragons though.'

'What about in the car?' asked Archie.

'It has voice-recognition software installed. I can read everything that is being said inside that car on

249

a monitor at the front.'

'So I can't make you forget everything,' said Dirk.

'Believe me, I have no interest in any of this. Let me take Mr Buchanan back. He needs medical attention. You have my word that I'll destroy his evidence and do my best to keep him away from dragons in the future. I've never liked this project.'

'I can't see that we have much choice,' said Dirk.

Buchanan staggered over to where Callum was crouched at Vainclaw's feet, stroking his legs.

'Where is the music?' he said to the boy.

'I've heard it too. My master used to sing to me, now he hears it himself,' replied Callum.

'The monsters have gone,' said Buchanan.

'The monsters are all around us,' replied Callum.

'Take the boy back too,' said Dirk. 'Send him back to his father.'

Weaver took Callum and Buchanan by the hand, led them back to the car, then looked back.

'I don't want my dad to work for Mr Buchanan any more,' said Holly.

Weaver nodded. 'I'll make sure he gets a fair redundancy deal.'

'Make sure you destroy all the evidence, Jonnie,'

called Ladbroke.

Weaver nodded, got in the car and started the engine.

'Is that his name?' said Holly.

'Yes,' said Ladbroke.

'How do you know?' asked Archie.

'The Department knows a lot of things,' replied Ladbroke. 'Unofficially, of course. Officially we know nothing.'

'What department?' said Dirk. 'Who are you?'

'My name is Pi Blandford.'

He held up a card for them all to see. In bold black capitals it read:

AGENT PI BLANDFORD
Department of Defence against anything that does not conform to the conventional understanding of the world as we know it
DODAATDNCTTCUOTWAWKI

Archie and Dirk barely had time to read it before the words faded and vanished, leaving an empty blank card.

'You're not called Ladbroke?' said Holly.

'If it helps, Ladbroke is one of my favourite names,' he said.

'And you know about dragons?' said Holly.

'Technically, no, the Department doesn't know anything about anything,' said Ladbroke, 'because the things we investigate do not technically exist.'

'Isn't that a bit weird?' said Archie.

'What's weirder? Pretending dragons don't exist or knowing that they do?' said Ladbroke.

'So you knew right from the beginning?' Holly said.

'When I first got assigned responsibility for dragons, I found a copy of Mr Klingerflim's book. I decided to check out his widow's house. That was when I discovered Dirk. When I saw you go round, Holly, I followed you home. Listening in on your phone conversations I learnt that your stepmother wanted to hire someone to follow you so I made sure that she found another of my cards.'

Ladbroke held out a cream-coloured card that read:

LADBROKE BLAKE
BLAKE INVESTIGATIONS:
Confidential, Professional and
Affordable Private Investigations

'Why have you never let on you knew before?' said Holly.

'The Department has a policy of non-intervention. I'm not supposed to get involved. My job is only to collect information on dragons.'

'Well, I'd hardly call this non-intervention, Mr Blandford. You're surrounded by dragons and you're talking to one,' said an elderly female voice behind him. 'I'm not sure you're within departmental guidelines.'

'Mrs Klingerflim,' said Holly, running to help the old lady out of the car and noticing the nasty purple bruise under her eye.

'Hello, dear. Hello, Archie. Hello, Mr Dilly.'

'So Ladbroke brought you here?' said Dirk.

'He was kind enough to fly me over,' said Mrs Klingerflim. 'We only arrived today, didn't we, Mr Blandford?'

'I wanted to know why Buchanan had brought Holly to Los Angeles,' said Ladbroke. 'I did a little research and learnt about the Summit of Skull Rock. There were no details in our case files, except for the names of those involved – Ivor and Elsita Klingerflim.'

'Elsita?' said Holly.

'That's my name, dear,' said Mrs Klingerflim. 'You didn't think my first name was Mrs, did you?'

Ladbroke continued. 'My contacts at NAPOW informed me that Buchanan was turning the library into some kind of trap. My contacts at the electricity board told me that the substation had gone down, so I dropped by and opened the roof for you. I never had any contact with you directly, so I didn't really break any rules.'

'Is that why you left Mrs Klingerflim to get out of the car and confront the Kinghorns on her own?' asked Dirk.

'No,' said Mrs Klingerflim. 'I told Mr Blandford to stay inside in case they used Dragonsong. Good thing too.'

'Now, Mr Dilly, I'd appreciate your thoughts on what to do about this situation,' said Ladbroke. He gestured to the nine dragons, looking like models in a waxworks museum.

'Leave them to me,' said Dirk. 'Will you make sure Holly and Archie get home safely?'

'The whole family will be flown home courtesy of the Department.'

'I owe you my life, kiddo,' Dirk said to Holly, and they hugged.

'When will we see you next?' said Holly.

'Very soon,' replied Dirk.

'It's been a pleasure never having met you, Mr Dilly,' said Ladbroke, shaking Dirk's paw.

Chapter Thirty-Four

After saying his goodbyes, Dirk watched the black car drive away into the darkness then turned to look at the three Desert Dragons, the two Scavenger brothers, the Sea Dragon, Vainclaw, his nephew, Jegsy, and the yellow-bellied, coal-black Cave Dweller, all frozen with the same faraway look in their eyes.

'Fairfax Nordstrum,' said Dirk, looking at him. 'Don't worry, you'll be back behind bars soon enough. Only this time, I'll have a word with Captain Karnataka and make sure you're convicted alongside these other Kinghorns.' Dirk looked at the rest of the dragons and smiled grimly. 'I know none of you can hear a word I'm saying now, but in a minute, you will.

After I've sung a little Dragonsong you'll all do exactly as I say when I tell you to turn yourselves in.'

Dirk stood back and opened his mouth to sing. He hesitated. His mother had been killed while under the influence of Dragonsong. He hated it. It was against the law to use it as a weapon, but he could think of no other way of resolving the situation.

Nine dragons stood frozen in front of him.

Nine sets of yellow eyes stared blankly ahead.

Then one set blinked.

Before Dirk could react, Fairfax Nordstrum's mouth opened and he felt a burning sensation as black flames shot out. The Cave Dweller leapt forward and landed forcefully on top of Dirk, his claws digging into his skin.

'Here's something interesting,' he said in a low voice. 'Did you know that the older the dragon the shorter the effects of Dragonsong last? I'm guessing not, otherwise you might have cut your speech short. I'm an old dragon, Mr Dilly.'

Dirk wrestled a leg free and kicked Fairfax off him, leaping up and diving at him, claws drawn. Fairfax evaded his attack and swung his tail at Dirk, but Dirk rolled out of the way and the tail smacked into Sorrentino's face, knocking him out of his stupor. Dirk jumped to his feet but too slowly. Fairfax was on top of him, pinning him down.

'So, Dirk Dilly, the dragon detective,' said Fairfax. 'Traitor to your species, my black fire will melt your pathetic brain. Do you have any last words?'

Dirk looked into Fairfax's cruel yellow eyes. He could feel the heat from his breath but he was helpless to stop him. 'I guess it's true,' he said. 'The bad guys do get their fair share of winning too.'

'Sorrentino, come and watch me kill this dragon,' said Fairfax. 'Sorrentino?'

Suddenly Fairfax's face contorted with pain. He let out a scream so loud that it seemed to fill the empty desert with noise.

Dirk felt the weight lift off him as Fairfax fell to the ground, screaming, twisting in pain and lashing out in desperation. 'What is this?' he cried.

Dirk stood up and saw on Fairfax's black back a patch of sticky green liquid hissing, burning its way through his thick scaly skin. Behind him, Sorrentino wiped his mouth.

'Thank you,' said Dirk. 'But I thought you worked for him.'

'I'm off the clock,' said Sorrentino. 'Besides, I like my life just the way it is. I don't need no Kinghorn messin' things up, startin' wars.'

Fairfax writhed in agony as the poison tore through his body. He lashed out, limbs flying in all directions, catching Leon with his tail, sending him smacking into his brother, who, in turn, barged into Jegsy and Flotsam.

'Boss, what's wrong?' said Flotsam.

'Help me,' shouted Fairfax.

'Come on, boss,' said Flotsam, grabbing Fairfax and dragging him on to a large piece of flat rock. He uttered a few words in Dragonspeak and the rock drew the two of them down, closing over their heads, muffling the sound of Fairfax's screams.

Jegsy awoke Vainclaw with a smack in the face. The dark Mountain Dragon looked around. 'I don't know what's happened here,' he said with a deep growl, 'but now let us finally rid ourselves of this turbulent detective.'

Dirk stepped back, trying to work out the best way to fight the four dragons. The Kinghorns advanced.

'I don't think so,' said Sorrentino, leaping over them and landing next to Dirk.

'I'll make it worth your while not to get involved in this, Sorrentino,' said Vainclaw.

Sorrentino remained where he stood.

'Very well, we will destroy you both,' said Vainclaw.

'I thought I already explained that out here in the desert we fight fair,' said Kitelsky, and he and Putz landed next to Dirk and Sorrentino, claws drawn, spikes splayed.

Vainclaw sent a burst of fire forward and the Kinghorns attacked, but this time the Desert Dragons worked as a team. Putz grabbed Kitelsky's forearms and swung him round, smacking Leon and Mali sideways. While they were still reeling, Sorrentino flew over and came down hard on Vainclaw's head. Jegsy tried to help his boss but Putz swiped him with a claw. Leon roared fire at Sorrentino but he ducked and the fire caught Mali straight in the face.

'Watch it, bro,' said Mali.

Vainclaw attempted to send another burst of fire at Sorrentino, but Putz was on him, jabbing his claws into his back.

In fact the Desert Dragons were fighting so well, instinctively reading each other's moves, working together, that Dirk stepped back from the fight and watched. The Kinghorns were losing ground. It was only a matter of time before Vainclaw cried, 'Kinghorns, retreat. We'll save this fight for another day.'

Finally defeated, Vainclaw and the Kinghorns ran to

the rocks, spoke quickly and vanished into the ground.

'Nice job,' said Dirk.

'Now, that's what I call a rumble,' said Kitelsky.

'Yeah, they won't be coming back here in a hurry,' said Putz.

The flight back to England was distinctly less glamorous than the flight over had been. Ladbroke had pulled some strings to get round Archie's lack of passport but instead of Buchanan's luxury jet, they flew on an ordinary plane full of ordinary people, crammed in like sardines.

'I still don't understand why Brant made me redundant,' said Mr Bigsby, moving his elbow out of the way of the stewardess, who was coming down the aisle with the duty-free trolley.

'Don't complain, Malcolm,' said Big Hair. 'With the redundancy money he's given you we'll be able to do whatever we want. You could even set up your own business.'

Holly and Archie were in the seats behind them. The seatbelt sign went off and they twisted round to kneel on their seats. Behind them Mrs Klingerflim was snoozing next to Ladbroke Blake. He leant forward and said quietly, 'She fell asleep as soon as we sat down.'

'Will she be OK? It was a nasty fall,' said Holly.

'Don't worry. She's tougher than she looks. I'll keep an eye on her,' replied Ladbroke.

'What I don't get,' said Archie, 'is that Buchanan said he got the idea to set a trap when he heard Holly talking about the film, but wasn't it his idea to steal the film in the first place?'

'No,' said Ladbroke. 'Chase Lampton hired Sorrentino.'

'Chase? Why?' said Holly.

'He knew that the movie was going badly and the studio had told him that if he made one more flop they were going to drop him. He had a problem, so he phoned Sorrentino for a solution. Sorrentino told him to take his cameras to the desert.'

'But how would a film of dragons help?' said Archie.

'From what I've gathered Chase believed that people in Hollywood are easily distracted. His plan was to reveal the footage the same week that Petal's film was released, and while everyone was inviting him on chat shows to talk about dragons, Petal's film would go unnoticed.'

'Would that really have worked?' asked Holly doubtfully.

'Who knows? But I can see how people might be

more interested in the fact that there are dragons in the desert than in a rubbish film about a pop star's daughter. Eventually, Chase planned to reveal that the whole thing was an elaborate hoax, by which time he would already be making his next film and everyone would be left wondering how he made such realistic special effects. I think he was hoping to get an action movie off the back of it.'

'But it wasn't a hoax,' said Archie. 'The dragons were real.'

'Chase didn't know that,' said Ladbroke, pouring himself a drink. 'He thought Sorrentino was giving him a brilliant fake. He never dreamt that the footage would be real.'

'What if someone went looking for them in the desert?' asked Holly.

'Sorrentino would have told Putz and Kitelsky to hide out until the whole thing blew over.'

'So if Sorrentino was doing it for Chase, who stole the film?' asked Archie.

'Sorrentino,' said Ladbroke. 'When no one was looking, he decided to take the film so he could charge Chase more for it.'

'But he didn't sell it to Chase?' said Holly.

'No, he got a better offer,' replied Ladbroke, opening

a packet of free nuts and chucking a couple into his mouth. 'After hearing you telling Dirk about it on the phone, Buchanan told Hunter and Frank to acquire the film, whatever the cost. Then Sorrentino got greedy. He sold it to them for loads more money than Chase was willing to pay.'

'Chase can't have been happy.'

'He wasn't. First he accused Theo of working with Sorrentino. Then he kept phoning Sorrentino, calling himself Mr Tanner, which is the name of a character from one of his films, apparently. Eventually Sorrentino promised to do the only thing left to save Petal's film. He set fire to the rushes.'

'But won't they just make it again?' said Archie.

'No. After all the bad publicity, World Studios has decided to leave it. The funny thing is that it turns out that because of the insurance payout, *Petal – The Movie* is Chase's biggest success in years financially. He's already got a new film in production. It's called *Alien Cats Go Digital*.' Ladbroke snorted with laughter.

Holly and Archie laughed too.

'Talking of films,' said Ladbroke, pulling a set of headphones from a plastic bag, 'if you don't mind, I'm going to watch a movie. I'll speak to you later.'

Holly and Archie sat back down in their seats and

flicked through the films on offer on the monitor in the seat in front.

'What do you fancy watching?' asked Archie.

Holly looked at the options. 'Hey, *The Big Zero*,' she said. 'That's the one Dirk said was Chase's best film. Let's see what it's like.'

They both put on their headphones and the opening music began.

Soon they would arrive back in London and they would have to deal with school and Archie's mum and all the other bits of reality they had avoided thinking about on holiday. But for the moment they lost themselves in the film.

The screen showed an aerial view of Los Angeles. The camera moved in and a gruff voice spoke over the music.

'In some stories,' said the voice-over, 'the kind they like to tell you in Hollywood, the good guys always win and the bad guys always lose. Well, I live in the real Hollywood and I can tell you that in real life it ain't like that. In my experience, the bad guys get their fair share of winning too.'

Holly thought of Dirk and how she had almost lost him. She wondered how he was getting home.

The white shutter was pulled over the window,

otherwise she might have noticed, if she had looked very carefully, the outline of the tip of a claw belonging to a four-metre-long (from nose to tail), red-backed, green-bellied, urban-based Mountain Dragon, clinging to the top of the plane, perfectly blended with its paintwork, enjoying the free ride back home.